BRIDE FOR A CHAMPION

I command you to marry the bearer of this letter . . . Lady Alice Martinswood has no choice but to obey her dead father's final instruction. His choice is his champion, the mercenary Simon Paton, still haunted by the bloody sack of Constantinople. But on their wedding night, Simon mistakes Alice's tears of joy for those of anguish. Swearing not to hurt her again, he decides he must not touch her — a promise he finds impossible to keep, especially when Alice vows to beguile him . . .

Books by Lindsay Townsend
in the Linford Romance Library:

MISTRESS ANGEL

LINDSAY TOWNSEND

BRIDE
FOR A
CHAMPION

Complete and Unabridged

LINFORD
Leicester

First published in Great Britain in 2014

First Linford Edition
published 2015

A catalogue record for this book is available
from the British Library.

ISBN 978–1–4448–2265–6

Published by
F. A. Thorpe (Publishing)
Anstey, Leicestershire

Set by Words & Graphics Ltd.
Anstey, Leicestershire
Printed and bound in Great Britain by
T. J. International Ltd., Padstow, Cornwall

This book is printed on acid-free paper

1

I command you to marry the bearer of this letter. This is the man, the one I told you of, Alice, the one who saved me. My champion Simon Paton, come all the way from Constantinople. Marry him, bear him a son and heir and forget Henrietta. Do your duty by me.

Lady Alice, crouching on her knees with a cleaning rag and her missing sister's ribbon in one hand and her father's last letter in the other, knew she did not look her best. But what did that matter? Her father was dead and the dead no longer care for appearances. Since the loss of Henrietta, she did not care, either.

She glanced at the man's travel-stained

cloak and mud-splattered boots without looking up into his face. Her steward should not have brought the fellow into her presence, should have given her time to compose herself and greet him in the great hall, but she sensed Simon Paton had ordered otherwise.

And my steward obeyed him. Already my people take orders from him, because he is a man.

'Forgive my appearance, Lady Alice,' said the stranger in a deep, faintly accented voice, clearly indifferent to whether she forgave him or not. 'I had business to attend to in London. I have come as soon as I could.'

Alice dropped the yellow ribbon back into her sister's clothes chest. She had been searching the chest again for any sign that would point to where Henrietta had been taken and by whom, but her father's last letter contained a devastating order. *Marry him.*

The letter shook in her hand. Swiftly, she dropped it into the chest and closed the lid. 'Your name, sir?'

'I am Simon Paton. Your father's champion.'

The bearer of the letter. The man I am commanded to marry. 'You were with my father in London?' She almost choked on her next question, but she had to know. 'At the end?'

'I was, my lady. Your father died well and at peace.'

Alice wished she could cry. She longed for some relief. When word had come ten days ago of her remaining parent's death from fever she had expected to feel something. Instead her heart felt numb. Her beloved younger sister was lost to her and her father — their father — had disowned Henrietta weeks before. Henry Martinswood had always demanded absolute obedience from his daughters and, by her elopement, Henrietta had failed him. *Yet now, by letter, he orders me from the grave.* Marry this man. Give him sons. Do your duty. *Always obedience and no word of love. Our father never loved his girls.*

'My lady?'

3

Still without looking at Simon Paton directly, Alice reluctantly clasped his fingers and allowed him to draw her to her feet.

'My lady, you may be assured that your father died and is buried as he wished, in London.'

Beside the longed-for son that his London mistress had borne him, Alice guessed, wondering how this new knowledge did not pierce her soul. She had never met the young Henry, her father's namesake, but when the child had died two summers back Henry Martinswood had become still more cold and grim toward his daughters.

'Lady Alice. Look at me, Alice.'

Hearing her name said so gently, she looked up for the first time and stared, forgetting the tingling pins and needles in her legs, forgetting everything.

He was big, this Simon Paton, tall, well-made and starkly-handsome; black-haired and with a head-full of straggling, fierce curls. Tanned from many eastern suns, he was dressed in a mantle that was strange to her, very dark and at the same time glossy, like the plumage of a raven. His clean-shaven, pox-free face, as lean as a hermit's, thrust at her like the prow of a great ship.

He was smiling, or at least a shadow of a smile hovered round his full lips — though not his eyes. Simon Paton's eyes — a dark blue, almost black, ringed with curling black lashes — gazed at her in a coolly intense, measuring way, as if judging her. He had a contained energy in him, as if he was ready to wrestle with angels, yet at the same time found the challenge distasteful. An unhappy man, she thought, yet also a striving one.

The woman to win his heart will be most lucky. The idea — more a feeling than a thought — flashed through her and was gone, dashed aside by his next words.

'Alice, I understand your father's last wishes. I applaud them. Before he died, he spoke to me of them. When we are married, you will be safe. I shall protect you.'

Thoroughly disconcerted, Alice wrung her hand from his. 'He discussed my marriage with you?'

'To ask my consent.'

Yes, you are asked but I have to obey. It was the way of the world but she did not have to like it. 'And my consent?'

He waved that aside. 'You need a man to be safe. I agreed, subject to my seeing you.'

Alice clenched her teeth together, too proud to ask if he approved of her. Simon Paton was clearly enjoying her discomfiture.

'Shall we take a glass of wine or tisane together, my lady?' he went on smoothly. 'Toast our nuptials tomorrow?'

So soon? Alice dipped her head, afraid her face might show her alarm. 'Will you call my maid Beatrix, to serve us?' she asked this tall stranger — *my husband to be* — thinking he could be useful at least.

'Such duties are for a woman,' came back his curt response. 'I will await you here and we shall plan how best we shall manage together.' His dark eyes gleamed as she jerked her head up. 'How you will obey me.'

'You may be sure I shall be most agreeable,' Alice snapped, aggrieved afresh. 'I shall fetch a tisane.'

She withdrew, her head high and her heart hammering within her.

If he is so keen to marry me, might he also help me to find and recover Henrietta? Or will he be only too keen to gorge himself on my father's lands? Will this Simon Paton be thrilled with my dowry and delighted to keep me in my place? Such thoughts horrified her and she shivered. *Would I were a man, in command of my own fate!*

★ ★ ★

Simon watched Lady Alice stride from the chamber, kicking her long skirts and apron out of her way, much as she probably wanted to kick him. He almost called her back to make some apology, but then he thought of the

7

dead, deflowered, crushed womenfolk he had seen in Constantinople; women who would have wept to be as safe and pampered as this one. Fetching and serving little cups was women's work.

'Yet she is very fine,' Simon said aloud, surprising himself. 'Uncommonly pretty.' *Just in need of management, which is scarcely surprising, since her father is dead and she has no uncles or brothers. In Constantinople the Lady Alice would have learned to be more modest.* But Constantinople was fallen, a smoking ruin, and he had been unable to save it, or its women, or the children, those frightened screaming babies . . .

The reek of the destroyed, fired city hit him again like a spear thrust and he rocked briefly on his heels, glad that there was no one to see his weakness. Sharp Alice, with her moss-green eyes, would spot it though, so he must beware.

'My sister Henrietta is prettier.' She had returned and he had not heard her light footsteps, only her tongue, which could take a courtesy and twist it.

Without thought, he struck back.

'How is that possible, my lady? Will you tell me?'

Her green eyes darkened and her cheeks were suddenly tinged with a pale rose. Seeing her thus he felt ashamed of his unkindness but she answered him roundly, counting off the points as she handed him a cup of something hot and sweet-smelling off a wooden tray.

'First, my sister is younger and men always prefer young flesh. Second, she is taller and more ripely formed, with gold, not brown, hair and bright brown eyes, not old-leaf green. Third — ' She paused as she set the tray on top of an ancient chest and accidentally spilled some of the liquid in the flagon onto the lid of the chest. 'Henrietta is far less clumsy.'

She had changed what she had been going to say, he was sure of it, but she also smiled for the first time and he realized how young she was, surely no more than twenty. She was a little too thin and had shadows beneath her eyes that should not have been there, but she was still a youth. From the perspective of his seven and twenty years and his seasons of war and trouble, she was a child; a slender, very pretty girl, but still an infant.

And she has a younger sister, Henrietta. Why did my lord never speak of her? Where is she?

'Tell me of your sister,' he said. 'And what were you going to say just now?'

For an instant a gleam of teasing shone in her face, making her seem younger still, then she shrugged. 'Only that she is beautiful, uncommonly beautiful.'

Which may mean that the sister still has all her teeth. Simon took a sip of the tisane. To his surprise it was excellent and the fresh scent of strawberries drew him back to simple boyhood pleasures, before Constantinople. 'Good!' he remarked.

'Will you have bread and cheese also?' Alice asked, clearly falling into an accustomed role as hostess.

'The cheese,' Simon agreed, testing to see if the wench would obey him. 'I have a liking for cheese, so hurry along.'

'At once,' she answered, in a voice of frost. Certainly she was not clumsy in anger. Instead, in a fluid, graceful motion, she sped past him to the door again, her eyes glittering like a cat's. He met her stare for stare, wondering why he was troubling to tease — to break a girl's will was nothing.

But, lady or not, she should heed me. She needs a man to guide her.

'When you return you can tell me of your sister.' *Why had his lord never mentioned this Henrietta? Another daughter and the old man had never spoken of her.*

From the edge of his sight he saw Alice stop on the threshold, her shoulders and spine stiffening. She wanted to linger and talk now, he guessed, but she should learn to heed him.

'My cheese?' Simon waited for her to leave, but she twisted round like a spinning top, her long brown plaits flying, and said, very sweetly, 'I have news of Henrietta, something I learned this morning from going through her chest.'

'Nothing useful, I am sure,' Simon replied bluntly, wanting her to know he had seen through her obvious feint.

She smiled at him, her lips as lush as ripe cherries, and inclined her head, though she had not yielded yet. 'Perhaps, sir, you will escort me to the kitchen, then we may both return and tell all together?'

Her wish to have her own way amused him and he found himself happy to placate her. 'Aye, aye, I will go along with you,' he remarked, stretching his arms over his head. 'Let me see if you are a good little housekeeper.'

The girl's look of dismay at these words and more especially at his joining her in truth had Simon stalking to the threshold, where he held the door open. 'After you, my lady.'

The instant she stepped through and they were away from the chamber she barred the way through the narrow corridor with outstretched arms. 'What are you doing?' she hissed.

'I am your kitchen escort. Tell me, do you often wander alone and unattended?'

She ignored the question. 'You want cheese no more than I do, so why, really, are you here?'

'To ensure you are obedient, as a wife should be.'

In the dimly-lit, wood-paneled corridor he heard her snort, unless it was the passing hunting dog that sneezed.

'You dislike me?' Leaning against a wall, he allowed her to stop him for the moment. She was small and slim, brown as a sparrow, but for all that she was most gladdening to look on, with a beautiful face that could have graced a statue in Constantinople. 'Do you find men distasteful?' he added, to keep her still a little longer. *If she truly dislikes me and dislikes all men we shall have to reach another way of living together. I will not have her ground down.* His sudden sense of protectiveness toward

13

her surprised him.

Her expressive, mobile face at once became unreadable. 'I do not know you, so how can I say?'

'Yet you think me arrogant.' *Still, she does not flinch from me, so that is a start.* He played with the thought of leaning down and kissing her, to reinforce that idea, but knew that he stunk of horse and dusty roads.

Her breath stopped, as if she caught scent of him, or stifled a tart reply or a laugh — he was not sure which. She surprised him then by nodding her head and saying, in a considering way, 'Perhaps not, not for a champion.

'But,' she went on, 'whatever your opinion of me or my house-keeping, you will not keep me out of the search for Henrietta. She is my sister, not yours. I will not give up the search for her.' *Because of you* was her unsaid thought, driving between them like a blade of steel.

Exasperated — he did not give up on others either — he stepped closer, remembering other women, soft and vulnerable like this one, so defenseless at the last. 'You need protection.'

'And you need a woman's eye.'

'How is it I have never heard of Henrietta?'

She blanched at the question but answered promptly, 'My sister fancied herself in love and eloped, but since then I have had no word from her. Our father disowned her. He said she was dead to him.' Her voice dipped even lower. 'Henrietta is but fourteen.'

The old man disowned his fourteen-year-old child? Was he mad?

'I have to find her. I know my sister and how she thinks.'

'Do women think? And surely, if you know her so well, should you not have foreseen her elopement?'

Again, though, he spoke too harshly, as he might to men in a barracks. She flinched, as if struck, and he was sorry when tears misted her eyes. 'Alice, I am — '

He spoke to empty air. She had

turned and left him, speeding along the corridor and clattering down the stairs so that he had to jog to catch her. On the final step she whirled about and faced him. 'You will not bully me!'

Because he had clearly hurt her he raised both hands in a truce.

'Are we agreed?' she persisted.

'That you should be involved in her search and recovery? Not a bit,' he replied cheerfully, for how could he agree to that?

She pointed to his belt where his sword would be. 'No one is invulnerable, not even you, my lord.'

In the brighter light from the great hall, where even now servants and others were gathering, preparing for the later midday meal, her light brown hair was picked out with tiny flames of red, like threads of garnets. He savored the pert curves of her breasts rising and falling as she breathed her indignation. For an instant he wished he was like the earlier mercenaries of Constantinople and could Viking her away. He wished he had kissed her in the upper corridor, too, for was that not the reason he was here, to wed and bed this pretty nag?

'God is, I believe,' he replied mildly, amused as she clapped her hands together in sheer irritation and strutted off toward the kitchen block, the swing of her hips revealing her as very much a girl, whether she liked it or not.

2

Alice was hurrying across the yard, conscious of Simon Paton striding behind her, when she heard Clement the house steward calling.

'Stop, my lady, I beg you! Hold a moment, I pray!'

What now? she thought, and halted, feeling the summer sun scorch the back of her neck and aware of Simon looming alongside. She glanced about for Beatrix, her maid, for the girl could direct him to his cheese, but she guessed the fellow would stay. Wiry Clement, in his new summer clothes and fresh cap with its foolish tassel, huffing and bursting with chatter, had made sure of that.

'My lady, such trouble. Please, you must come. Euphemia the bonds-woman is in your lower garden — '

'Where I said she might go,' Alice

dropped in, before Simon remonstrated with her for that.

'Yes, my lady, I know. You are always most generous to your former wet-nurse, as is fitting, but . . . ' Clement, standing before her, his pale, faintly bulging eyes skipping from her to her massive companion, removed his cap from his bald head and began to fiddle nervously with its tassel.

'What else, man?' barked Simon.

'Please do not harass my people.' Alice put a hand on his chest to stop him mowing her hapless steward into the cobbles of the yard. It was like laying her arm against a rock. 'All will be learned more smoothly without your interference. Clement, take your time,' she added.

But even as she sought to protect Clement, her steward had twisted about to face Simon more fully and was answering him, instead.

'Sir, Euphemia was gathering berries and Beatrix was with her in the lower garden . . . '

Which explained the lack of her maid, Alice thought.

' . . . and Euphemia decided to gather some sprays of budding apples for a luck-charm . . . '

'That is wasteful,' remarked Simon.

'The trees are in need of pruning,' Alice said. 'Go on, Clement.'

'Euphemia climbed up into one tree and her shoe became lodged in a crack and now she is stuck, and she is bleeding again and afraid, and I am most sorry, sir, my lady,' said Clement in a rush, gasping.

Simon glanced down at her, his tanned face a mask of puzzled disapproval, but Alice shook her head. 'I will see to this.'

'Bleeding again?' Simon barred her flight with an arm. 'This has happened before?'

Alice felt herself flush. ''tis nature, that is all,' she said gruffly. 'Euphemia is older and sometimes when a woman is older her monthly times — '

He dropped his arm. 'Go to her. She

20

knows you well and will heed you.'

She was about to, but it was irritating to be ordered.

Her maid Beatrix, tall and angular, her bright chestnut hair her single claim to beauty, finally appeared at the postern gate of the yard. Before Simon could order her, too, Alice hastened to meet her.

'Beatrix, this is Simon Paton,' she told the startled woman, before Beatrix could speak. She pointed over her shoulder, exasperated afresh as she saw her maid's hazel eyes widening in approval. 'Please find him some cheese and other victuals and go with him to my chamber. I shall be as swift as I can.'

Alice hurried down to the postern gate, realizing too late she had not bid her future husband farewell — no doubt another mark against her.

Do I care? she wondered, feeling her way down the narrow stone steps that plummeted to the lower garden. She could not see Euphemia in the apple trees, but she could hear a lusty weeping amidst the branches.

'I am here, dear heart,' she called out. 'I am here and all shall be well. Hang on, Euphemia, and I will get you safely down.'

'I am bleeding unto death!' cried a wavering voice, and the branches of the largest apple tree shook.

'Away with you all,' Alice told a knot of round-eyed pages, sending them scampering up the steps toward the house. She had enough to do for her sobbing former nurse, without their avid interest.

She ran along the grassy garden path and found Euphemia stuck in the largest apple tree, red-cheeked, flushed and weeping, as she often was these last few months, poor creature. Her former wet-nurse was a buxom, fair woman who until this last year had been easy-going and good natured. Now as her monthly women's courses faltered and stuttered due to her increasing age, Euphemia was a victim of wild emotions and wilder fancies. When she was in such a state few could deal with her, except Alice.

So I must coax the poor woman and comfort her and I am glad to do it, but why must it be now? Finally I have someone I can speak to about Henrietta — and, pray God, Simon will be willing to help me — and still I must delay.

The injustice burned in her, so she was most careful not to let any grain of anger seep into her voice. It would not do to take out her frustration on another weaker than herself.

'Dear heart,' Alice called up to her, stripping off her rough apron from around her middle. 'It is your monthly course flooding a little, as it has before.' She held up her apron. 'I shall climb up and free your foot and you can wear this around your hips.'

A loud sniff told Alice her calm, practical tones had worked. Euphemia was calming a little. 'My lady?'

Alice glided to the foot of the tree and looked up into the crown of branches. Euphemia's round, unhappy face peeped down to her through a haze of twigs and leaves and busy spiders. Alice smiled at her and patted her belt of keys. 'When we are back at the house we shall visit the buttery,' she promised. 'I have something I hope you will taste for me. Will you pass down your boughs?'

That request brought on a fresh onslaught of weeping. Through the storm, Alice learned that Euphemia could not, *could not*! The wicked tree had snatched her foot and now she was stuck forever.

'Roger would not let that happen,' said Alice. 'Your husband loves you dearly. And Thomas.' To mention Euphemia's son Thomas, who had gone off into the wickedness of Oxford, as Euphemia called that city, was always a risky undertaking. Now, however, her former nurse gave a loud sniff and announced she had received word from Tom that morning. He was happy as an apprentice tanner, and doing well.

Alice praised Tom and was heartened

when the few cut branches were passed down to her. They were making progress.

'I am climbing up. Do not fret — the tree can carry us both.'

From childhood she had climbed and these trees were familiar to her. Remembered hand-holds returned to her memory and she scampered into the low-arching apple tree like a squirrel, soon coming alongside Euphemia. The maid's skirts were slightly bloodied at the back, she noticed, but luckily Euphemia did not know it. For the rest, her former nurse looked full of good humors and now had a bright color, so she would be unlikely to faint.

A quick glance at her foot, trapped in a fork in the tree trunk, showed that it was indeed snared fast. She would need to ease it free, and for that Euphemia would need to be calm.

'Well now, how far we can see from here,' Alice said, by way of greeting, rocking slightly on her branch so Euphemia might feel the motion. 'Do you remember how we would all come here when Henrietta was tiny? How she loved trying to catch the apple blossom?'

The memory, told to comfort Euphemia, had the opposite effect on herself. In a flash, she recalled her sister only a year ago, walking arm in arm with her in this garden. Henrietta had been thirteen then, tall and gracious as an empress and filled with plans — how she would become a nun, how she would learn to make the best ale in Oxfordshire, how she would breed war-horses and go on crusade . . .

Alice blinked a mist from her eyes and realized Euphemia was saying something. 'I beg your pardon?'

'Clement is back again. He is bringing someone, a very tall, handsome gentleman. Oh! And he will see me here, trapped by the tree and bleeding to death!'

'It does not show,' Alice reassured, 'and if we are nimble we may free you first.' She wanted to be out of the apple tree before Simon appeared. Gripping a branch, she reached down to Euphemia's foot, fumbling to undo her shoe.

'He is very comely,' her former nurse continued, diverted out of her fear by the stranger. 'Is he the one who saved the master from thieves last month in London?'

Alice gripped Euphemia's narrow, arched foot and tugged gently.

'Ow!' said the maid, as her foot, and its shoe, came loose.

'You are scratching her that way,' drawled a knowing voice. 'She needs bringing down from the other side.'

A short noonday shadow flitted around the trunk of the tree and then Simon was reaching up, cradling Euphemia into his long, muscular arms and lifting her free. Alice saw Euphemia's dazzled face and knew she had just lost another possible ally. Her former nurse, giggling slightly with her head resting against her husband-to-be's shoulder, would be all for him now.

Rapidly, so he could not paw her out of the tree, Alice scrambled down. She landed with a jolt that had her nipping her tongue with her teeth, a smarting blow that made her whole jaw ache and her eyes smart. Determined not to be seen on the verge of tears, she scooped up the branches Euphemia had collected as Simon swept by, carrying her maid as if she was as light as a cobweb.

'I think it best to return to the house, yes?' he asked, pausing until she glanced up at him.

'Yes,' Alice mumbled, wondering if she had blood in her mouth and if so where she might spit. She forced herself to swallow instead, feeling faintly sick and thoroughly disheartened.

'Stay here,' Simon told her, when they reached the bottom of the narrow garden steps. 'We must speak together a moment.'

'My maid — '

'Others will tend her,' came the brutal response. He motioned to Clement to take the cut apple boughs, which, to Alice's intense annoyance, her steward did without a sound. 'You wait.'

Like saying 'Stay' to a hound!

She did stay, but only because Beatrix rushed to her down the steps, her thin face taut with distress. 'My lady, I did try to do as you asked.'

With a further sinking heart, Alice knew what she was going to say.

'I took the lord back to the chamber, but then the gentleman said I might leave and so I had to go.' Beatrix unwound some thread distractedly off her spindle and wound it on again. 'He said you would need me, my lady.'

Alice nodded and patted the maid's arm. 'No matter,' she said, feeling her blood boiling like hot oil. 'Will you stay with Euphemia? Take her to the buttery and let her try the new cordial. You try it, also.'

She waved aside Beatrix's thanks and then pelted back into the lower garden, running as if with hunting hounds. If the wretched man demanded she wait here then she would, but he would have to find her, too.

3

Simon, finally detaching himself from the gaggle of maids and pages, strode back to the lower garden. When he did not spot Alice at once, sitting on the steps or wandering the small paths, he grunted and plunged on into the tangle of budding fruit bushes.

She would make it hard to track her, he guessed, but he had a cure for that and no time to waste on her girlish folly. A small part of him was vastly amused, but he strove to ignore it.

'Ach!' He slapped the side of his neck as if stung and stumbled onto the path, crouching as if he had fallen. Now he was down, he settled himself comfortably amidst the spent cowslips and primroses — flowers from his childhood that he had forgotten.

He was watching a hover fly, hanging in the sultry July air, when he heard an explosion of twigs behind him. Alice rushed out from behind a medlar bush and skidded to a stop.

She narrowed her green eyes at him and he chuckled. 'Will you sit a moment with me, my lady? Now you know I am unhurt?'

She tapped her foot on the green earth. 'A deceiver and a bully, Sir Simon?'

Enjoying her indignation, he lay back on his elbows, thinking he did have a few moments to tease her after all. 'Master Simon, or Simon, if you please, my lady. I am no English knight.'

'No, you are a mercenary.' She spat the final word as if it burned her.

'We do not all have lands and titles. I protect others and am paid for doing so. Is that so evil, my lady?'

'Alice, please, just Alice, if I must call you Simon.' She tapped her foot again, glancing back toward the house, and chewed on her lower lip. 'Did my father ever speak of Henrietta?'

'No, and that is why we must talk.'

He smiled at her raised brows, thinking how comely she was when caught in surprise, her soft little mouth slightly open.

She tossed her rough apron on the grass and knelt on it. 'What changed your mind Simon?'

'You are sisters,' he said simply. 'She may have told you more.'

She sat back on her heels, clearly unaware that she had a twig stuck in her veil. 'And if I have information, will you share yours?' She leaned forward, intent as a stalking cat. 'Do you know how frustrating it is to know nothing and be told nothing? Yes, yes, I am a woman and the sphere of action is that of men, but Henrietta was stolen away by a man.'

'And you think, in justice, men should include you?'

She looked surprised again, but nodded quickly.

It had been his intent to coax any womanish confidences from her and then act on them, but now he saw a little of how it must be for her.

'Has she written to you at all?'

'Not of late. It has been several months, and no word. It is not like her to be so silent. Her last letter to me was dated the second of April.'

This was ten or eleven days before the fall of Constantinople, when he had been fighting to keep the city free from invaders. Quickly, Simon closed his mind to that and thought of this young woman's sister. With Henrietta only fourteen and missing, and a harsh, absent father lately dead, it was no wonder that Alice was slender, with shadows under her eyes.

His impulse to embrace her surprised him, but he contented himself by smoothing the twig from her short veil. 'May I see her letter?'

Swiftly, Alice brought out a much-handled scrap of parchment from her bodice and handed it to him. Simon read it carefully and returned it to her with thanks.

'She seems much in love with this

Edward,' he observed. 'Do you know anything of him, his family, his status? Is he French or English? Will your sister now be in England or France?'

'I do not know!'

The words seemed wrung from her. After a moment she shook her head. 'You saw her letter,' she went on hesitantly. 'It is all how she feels, how happy she is, how handsome Edward is, and what he says to her.' She tugged at the grass in a distracted fashion. 'I wish she had told me something more, his family name, where he is from, anything useful. I think she said once he is a squire.'

'Whose?' If he had a name he could make progress.

'I do not know,' she said a second time, more quietly, as if the enormity of the search overwhelmed her.

'And you had no warning that she would elope with him?'

She gave him a look of scorn which he admitted he deserved.

'Has she friends of her own age she

may have spoken to?'

'No. For the last year she has been at the court of Queen Eleanor overseas. I was glad for her to go. She was too young to be stuck in the country, spending her days making possets and tisanes and waiting for our father to visit from London.'

So are you, thought Simon, but he let that pass.

'Your father was happy with the arrangement?' he asked.

'Oh yes, Father has met the queen and knows her court.'

Queen Eleanor was famous for her love of learning, poetry and courtly manners. Simon had heard stories of the ladies of her court sitting in disputation as to the nature of love — an absurd idea to him, but no doubt appealing to a girl of fourteen. 'Courts of love?' He asked quietly. 'A young girl alone?'

'That was a long time ago,' said Alice quickly. 'And Henrietta was with her aunt and uncle and in their household, so my father thought her safe enough.' She tugged at more grass. 'If we find and recover her, it is only justice that Henrietta should have the lands and dowry that is due to her, my lord. Then, pray God, she might seek a bridegroom worthy of her.'

And if Henry Martinswood were still alive he would not have chosen a former mercenary from Constantinople as a husband for you, my girl, Simon thought, but he said nothing, merely marking Alice's use of 'my lord' in her plea. *She cannot know I would never cheat her sister out of her rightful inheritance.* As for the rest, time and Fate had worked against Henry Martinswood, but his former lord had done the best he could for his elder daughter, except —

'Why are you not already married?' he demanded. 'You are what age, eighteen, nineteen?'

She glared at him again. It was like being caught in a cold, bracing shower. 'Why are you not married?' she demanded in return.

'I never found a lass who would be interested in a landless fighter,' he said calmly. 'And you?'

She tore up another handful of grass. 'I want to be more to a man than simply my lands.'

What part of faery are you dwelling in? he almost said, but there was no need to be cruel. 'Is Henrietta a spirited creature?'

'Like me, you mean? No, my sister is very gentle, when she has her own way, and always sees the good in everyone.'

When she has her own way. Chiefly to reassure Alice, Simon asked, 'What if she is right? Perhaps Edward is kindly and loving and they are safely married.'

'May it be so! But I dislike the timing.'

Simon lifted his hands and she needed no more encouragement.

'Queen Eleanor died in the spring and Henrietta vanished from her court soon after, days after, I suspect. I think Edward, whoever he is, has plotted her disappearance most carefully. I dread he might be a schemer. My aunt and uncle know nothing. No one at the queen's court knows anything.'

'Or if they do, they are not saying.'

Still kneeling back on her heels, she punched the grass. 'Exactly!'

Though her words and gestures were brave, he saw her tremble slightly. 'Have you heard any word of your sister since Henrietta's last letter?'

She nodded. 'A man came from the king last month, with a scribe, to consider adding my name to a list of heiresses. At least, he said he was from the king,' she added doubtfully.

Simon felt a chill of suspicion. 'Go on.'

'He mentioned my sister, said he had seen her at Christmas at the court of the old queen. I asked him about Edward.'

'You asked, rather than your father?'

She flushed and stared at a daisy to avoid looking at him. 'Father would not speak of Henrietta. He said she was dead to him. I spoke to the herald alone.'

There was a tense silence between them, filled by the droning of a bumblebee. Staggered by what she had just admitted, Simon wondered what he would have done, had he been in her place. For Henry Martinswood to cast Henrietta aside was more than harsh, it was cruel.

After a moment, Alice sighed and went on. 'The king's man, if he was such, claimed he knew nothing of any Edward, but he half-smiled as he said it. I think he does know more, but he left the same day. A small, stocky man, with a smiling mouth and mean eyes. Sir Bohemond de Lyonesse.'

'That name I recognize, even from Constantinople!' Simon cracked his fists together, a sudden fizz of excitement coursing through his veins. 'All Bohemonds are ambitious and he is no different, but soft as a copper spoon. King's man or not, he will hang around the royal court still as such men always do. I will find him, persuade him to say more. I know de Lyonesse's haunts of old, where he will have gone to ground.'

Her face began to drain of color again as she lifted her head to face him. 'Do you think this Edward and Bohemond somehow acted together?'

'I have a name and a man to go after, which is all that matters.' Simon spoke heartily, although he suspected she might be right. Still, he did not want to alarm her any more, since she was already as pale as parchment. He changed the subject slightly.

'You say King John has a list of heiresses?'

'The king takes great notice of any wards or heiresses who might come into his care if or when their parents are dead.'

He looked at her still, wary face, guessed she disliked the King's obsession, but dismissed it from his mind. *No matter, since we are to be wed.*

'Why not appeal to the king to find your sister?'

She gave an energetic shake of her head. 'I think his terms would be too high. Besides — '

'You hope to avoid scandal and discover her first.'

Alice stared at the daisy again. 'Of course.'

'And yet you see a man like Bohemond de Lyonesse alone, unattended, after all that has happened?'

He had been thinking of Greek maids, closely sequestered, that was the trouble, and he spoke again without thought. The instant the words were out he regretted them, but it was too late.

'No!' She was already on her feet, spitting her denial. 'You gull me into a confidence, into speaking with you freely and then you scold! That is unfair!'

As Alice spoke she was moving, but so was he. When she stumbled at the very start of her headlong dash back up the garden, he caught her, clutching her tight. He was afraid for an instant that she would fall flat on her face in her haste to escape him.

She squirmed in his grip, as fast and

furious as an angry falcon bobbing and bating on a hunter's wrist, struggling with its jesses. 'Release me, raptor!'

The insult burned him — he who had seen so many women raped and murdered at the fall of Constantinople and been unable to save them. 'I am none such,' he began, through gritted teeth, breaking off as he felt her attempting to unwind his fingers off her waist.

Almost as if she sensed his attention she stopped at once and looked straight into his face, her eyes as bright as eastern jade. 'If you were a true gentleman, you would let me go.'

'I am a mercenary.'

Without a flicker, she returned: 'As a Christian, you should not treat me so rudely.'

What did she know of what one Christian might do to another? But he would not back down. If he was to marry this salamander then she must learn, and the lesson would begin now, whether he stank of horse or not.

He tightened his grip around her narrow waist, crossing his hands in the small of her back. As he inhaled her lavender scent and felt her lissome body mold against his, he was dimly aware of her standing up on her tip-toes. Before he realized what she was about, she had kissed him first.

He was so startled by the sudden tender sweetness of her mouth that he sighed, bringing a hand up now to smooth a tendril of her hair away from her sun-warmed cheek. She tasted of sugar cone and honey and, he fancied, cherries, although that might only be wishful thinking.

Her kiss went on, slow and sure, an instant of gentleness when he had known few such moments in his life, glowing in his mind like a rare flower or book. Her eyes were closed as she gave herself in her kiss, and he closed his eyes too, relishing the contact where their breaths mingled and their lips touched and touched and touched . . .

'Women can also kiss,' she murmured.

43

'I know.' He enjoyed the quiver her mouth made against his as they conversed in this unusual fashion. 'Is this because you like me, or because you wish to be first?'

He felt rather than heard her laugh. 'Too late for you to discover,' she teased. She started to step back, float off like a scrap of thistledown, but he was a fighter with a warrior's swiftness and reactions, and he gathered her back before she was gone. 'I do not think so,' he answered, and he kissed her again.

Alice fought herself. She strove to remember her sister, to escape from this heady world of sensation, where she felt higher than the clouds. She had anticipated Simon's kiss and intercepted it, bested it, but now she was losing. He had trapped her when she had expected to escape. Time and the world had stopped for her while she hung in his arms.

Foolish! Her mind raged, but how could she have known? She had never kissed a man before, not as couples kiss.

His tanned nose bumped lightly against hers and she felt him smile. Simon had not kissed often before, she sensed that and was pleased, but she had no chance to consider why that should be so, because his kiss deepened.

His mouth and tongue eased her mouth apart, feathering and caressing the tender, sensitive insides of her lips. He smelled of horses and dust, from travel, and his own musk and warm leather — a scent she would now recognize forever as his. His big, sword-callused palms were flat across her back, hugging and holding, but not presuming, not fingering lower. *He respects me*, she thought, bringing her arms about his middle, her breath stopping as he lifted her right off her feet.

'Sir, a messenger for you! Sir?'

Simon growled something in Greek, his grip tightening on her a moment before he set her back lightly on the path. 'More later, eh?' he murmured, touching her shoulder. Then he bowed, turned and ran back toward the steps and the tanned blond messenger, calling, 'What news, Alexios?'

4

It was time for the noonday meal, the public meal, when the lord or lady of the manor should see and be seen. Alice shifted slightly on her bench beside the great chair on the dais. Simon was outside in the yard, seeing off the mysterious messenger, whom she had not met. The great hall was filling up with men and women from her father's estate and men — recognizable by their tans and flowing robes — from Simon's retinue. There was a busy hum of conversation and the servers were rushing to and fro setting up the trestle tables below the dais. It was not a feast day but a few musicians, a troupe who had arrived that morning, were whispering in a corner and preparing to play their harps and rebecs. They had packed their pipes away. Surprised, Alice left her seat and crossed to them.

'You do not wish to play your pipes?' she asked, when greetings and their thanks to her were over.

'Oh, no, lady. The lord said he does not care for pipes.' Speaking, the eldest of the musicians pointed to the doorway, where Simon blocked out the sun briefly with his body as he crossed the threshold.

'Of course.' Alice forced a smile and hurried to Simon, conscious of her lips throbbing slightly, as they had after he had kissed her.

He looked surprised to see her gliding across the meadowsweet and other summer strewings to meet him, but she did not give him time to speak.

'Why no pipers?' She gestured to the musicians.

He grinned, his teeth showing astonishingly white in his tanned face. 'With pipes there are always drums. If we are to talk, do you want to pitch your voice over a battle-array of noise?'

He took advantage of her brief silence to offer her his arm and guide her to her seat.

'Thank you, that is most considerate.' Should she be thanking him? she wondered, distracted afresh when he waited for her to sit first on the dais, as a true knight and gentleman should. He took the lord's chair, she noted, aware that no one in the hall protested — including herself.

Are you so in awe of him already?

The musicians flourished a brief fanfare of sorts on their harps and Clement, now wearing his tasseled cap, stepped beside the unlit fireplace.

'My lady Alice and my lord Simon Paton are now at their meal!' he called in his stentorian steward's bellow. 'Join them, and be welcomed.'

So my people all know and have accepted Simon, even before we are wed. Alice was unsure if this knowledge comforted or confounded her.

'Did the messenger have news of my sister?' she whispered to her husband-to-be as the people in the hall took their seats on the trestle benches with much scraping of boots on the floor timbers and wails from one or two overexcited, hungry children. She liked children, and always allowed them within the hall.

'He did not.' Simon placed a trencher before her and gestured to the carver to begin serving her.

'Is that all?' Alice asked, thinking that despite their earlier talk and even their embrace, nothing had changed. He was still hoarding knowledge and shutting her out. *Just like my father.*

Disappointed and aggrieved, she wiped her mouth, trying to forget the tender closeness of his kisses and determined to protest.

Before she could do so, a man with the leather complexion and rangy walk of a shepherd marched before the high table. 'Lord, I demand justice, as is my right!'

The shepherd — Walter of Woodbury, Alice remembered — was looking at Simon, sitting in the high seat, and not at her. The musicians fell silent and everyone looked at Simon.

'These matters should wait for the

manorial court, Walter,' she began, but the man was having none of it.

'And when will that meet again with a lord present? Begging your pardon, Lady Alice, but there has been scant business at the manorial court these days.'

'Ha! You mean to dupe the stranger and to ignore my rights!' cried a strident voice, and another man hurled himself from one of the lower tables and threw himself at the shepherd. In a flurry of arms and legs the two men went down fighting and rolled like dogs on the herb-strewn floor.

Cursing in Greek, Simon leapt over the high table in a single, long-legged bound and closed on the pair. Alice snapped her fingers at a page carrying a pitcher of water meant for people to wash their hands, seized it and flung it at all three men, truly not caring who she hit.

The shock of the cold water stopped the scuffle. In the abrupt silence that followed and while the two peasants sat wiping their dripping faces, Simon stalked back to the dais.

'Madam, a private word, if you please?' His blue eyes blazing, his hand closed around hers under the cover of the table. Alice had no doubt that if she resisted he would drag her out publicly.

She submitted rather than create a new spectacle for which she was the main player. Leaving her half-served meal untouched, she nodded to Clement to carry on and walked from the great hall into the yard.

She did not say a word until they were passing the bathhouse, silent and dark at this hour. 'In here.' She could be as laconic as him.

He thrust open the door to the bathhouse and followed so close on her heels she could feel the heat rising off him, like a fresh-baked loaf. He stopped in the sunlight of the threshold. 'A rowdy household.'

'We cannot all have the luxury of cowed retainers.'

'Truly, do my men look groveling to you?'

She sighed and folded her arms before herself so she would not be tempted to hit out at him. Or was the temptation rather to press that dark mantle of his against his brawny chest? It was so damp it would reveal his every sinew and muscle.

'My clothes amuse you?'

She jerked her head up and met his dark blue eyes again. His face was as unreadable as a stone, but his eyes gleamed — with sympathy or scorn she could not tell. 'Say what you must and let me go back.'

'Give yourself a break from it today. Is it always so vigorous?'

Expecting him to remonstrate, she was startled for an instant before pride overcame her. Did he think she could not cope? 'I do not need pity!'

'Strange, I think all of us need compassion at times.'

Surprised, she took a deep breath and started again. 'Why did you manhandle me from the hall?'

A half-smile tweaked at his lips. 'I did

not think you would come with me. And, Alice, I did feel you needed . . . respite.' He frowned, touching the lintel of the bathhouse lightly with the tips of his fingers. 'I sense it has been worse since your father died. You should not have to struggle alone.'

She did not want to admit anything but felt the betraying blush steal up her face and knew he had spotted it — he saw everything to do with her.

She shook her head. 'I do not understand you.' At times he seemed arrogant, presumptuous, taking the lord's seat as a right, speaking to her as if she was a child, brazen in seeking to thrust her firmly into a woman's role of passive waiting. At other times, he was different. Her mind flashed to his gentleness with her maid and to his tender embrace, his beguiling, tormenting kisses.

'Which Simon are you now?' she demanded. 'The brutal, the disapproving, or the undoing?'

He laughed aloud, his roar of a chuckle echoing round the beehive walls of the bathhouse. 'Which would you have, Penelope?'

'Who is that? Why do you call me that?' Alice began, breaking off as Simon gathered her firmly into his arms. 'What are you doing?'

'She was a queen, long ago. A queen who had to struggle alone, as you have done.' He lifted her slightly and lowered her neatly so her feet rested on top of his. 'There, so the damp of this place does not spoil your shoes.'

She smiled and could not help it. 'How did her husband woo her, this Penelope?'

Simon felt the burning in his gut fade as she spoke. He did not know how to deal with her, that was the truth. In Constantinople he had been with courtesans, but other women were a mystery to him. He wanted Alice and she would be a pleasure to take to bed, but already, after less than a day of knowing her, he discovered he did not really want to fight with her. Not quarrel-fight, at least.

How do I woo her? He thought of the terror he had seen etched on the faces of other women, of Greek women, and swore then to himself that he would never do anything that would cause Alice to look at him like that. But he did not want to be too soft, either — Henry Martinswood, her father, had asked him to come here as his champion and her protector.

Hers and her sister's, wherever she is. Find Henrietta — she needs finding quickly.

'Simon?'

He liked the way she said his name but he could not recall what she had asked. She made him lose his wits after only a day, and if he was not careful she would wind him round her little finger like a silk ribbon. But perhaps he could even up that sweet tussle between them, make her feel as confounded as he was.

'What was it again? Brutal, disapproving, undoing?' he murmured, folding her more snugly against him. He still had not bathed in this primitive country, but for the moment he no longer cared if he smelled like a tinker from the road. 'Shall we see?'

Her green eyes were wide as he swooped in, fast as a hawk. He brushed her lips with his, swept on and nipped her ear lightly between his teeth. She giggled, unconsciously leaning into him more, and then she stiffened, as if startled by her own response.

She is an innocent, he warned himself. *Do not alarm her.*

Remember you should be seeking her sister, his conscience goaded, and Simon promised himself then and there that he would set out again soon, as soon as his horses were rested.

First there is Alice and our marriage —

'You are all wet from that pail.' He touched her sleeve at her wrist, then her elbow, then her shoulder, his fingers tracing higher and higher. 'Perhaps you should complete the process and take a bath?'

'With you?' Her voice was higher

than normal and he could sense her rapid heartbeat. His own heart was thumping, too.

She swallowed. 'Then we should be undone, Simon, both of us.'

Her eyes were so very large, yet trusting, and she did not squirm or fight in his arms. She hesitated before him, as if she too was uncertain how to act and did not know if she wished to flee or stay. But she had not tried to break from him.

And if I do nothing she will think me disinterested, or worse, only concerned with her lands.

He wanted to do more — already his loins were aching as they never had with the courtesans of the east — but he did not want her to be afraid.

Inspiration struck him. Placing his hands lightly on her shoulders — to keep her from stumbling off his boots, nothing more — he kissed her on the forehead. 'May I kiss you more?' he asked, his voice a growl with desire but as gentle as he could make it.

'If you will tell me what the

messenger said,' she began, then gave her head such a violent shake that her two hair plaits bobbed. 'No, I do not play that way,' she added, and, closing her eyes, she offered her mouth.

Softly, he traced the outline of her lips with his thumb and drew her back into his embrace. This time he took but she also gave, her tongue teasing as he plunged into the freshness of her kiss. This was nothing like the chaste kisses of a court or the deliberate, fast kisses of a courtesan, intent on stirring and arousing. Alice kissed him to know him, to allow him to learn her.

She touched his chest with the curled fingers of a hand and gave a tiny sigh. He mirrored her by caressing her narrow back, feeling her delicate spine and sleek flanks with the tips of his fingers. She extended her fingers and, through the damp, sticky cloth of his mantle, traced the curve of his ribs, one by one. Still he kissed her, even as her delicate, tentative caress concentrated his desire.

'We should stop.' She turned, laying

her head against his shoulder.

Hanging grimly onto his self-control by a thread, Simon could only agree. 'I will return to the hall,' he said.

At once her eyes, which had been dreamy and young, sharpened and focused. 'Alone, to show your mastery?'

He cursed her suspicious thoughts and his own carelessness. 'Alone, to give your people the justice they crave and so you can rest and prepare for our wedding day,' he answered, remonstrating with himself to be more patient. They were still near strangers to each other and it was natural that she would be wary. 'Believe me, Alice, you have the better of it.'

Unable to resist, he kissed her again and scooped her off her feet, carrying her out into the sunlit yard. 'I shall come when I may and after we are wed tomorrow, we shall discuss plans to find your sister.'

'We? Truly?'

He nodded, touched by her wondering voice and glowing look. He admitted to himself for the first time that as much as she longed to be part of any plan, he also needed her help. *How harsh her father has been with her and her sister! How cruel to dismiss Henrietta and to leave Alice so bereft, and for months. Henry Martinswood has done badly by her. I will do better.*

'We,' he said aloud.

5

Beatrix closed the door behind her as she left and Alice burrowed deeper into the bed, waiting for her new husband. Theirs had been a quiet wedding, both of them stiff and formal in their best clothes. For a dreadful instant she had feared Simon would say nothing about her gold-sheathed plaits or wide-sleeved blue and gold gown, but he had smiled at her by the church door and whispered, 'You look beautiful, my Alice.'

'You look amazing,' she had whispered back, which was true. Garbed in his shining blue-black mantle and a white tunic, shaved and scrubbed, he looked younger, more approachable. *Certainly no mercenary.* When he had grinned at her she dared to hope all would be well.

Now, as the evening lengthened and

the great hall below her chamber quieted, Alice began to be nervous. Was Simon drinking downstairs with his men? Would they all come up together as rowdy escorts? Was he a man who loved his drink? *Has Henrietta already endured something similar, and is she married?*

Alice sat up, rigid in bed, and froze as Simon entered, quietly and alone. He looked at her steadily, his handsome face still that of a stranger.

'Cold?' he asked her and she shook her head, too shy to speak. As was the custom, especially in summer, she was naked in bed and now horribly conscious of her nudity. *Does he think me too small, too slender, too pale?*

'I can fetch a brazier,' he went on, and she shook her head a second time.

'I have some sweets for us,' he said carefully, as if she were slow-witted. For the first time Alice realized he carried a tray, and on it were cups and a flagon and little dishes filled with morsels of food. Grateful for his care, she forced herself to speak.

'Any cheese there?' she asked, and he smiled at her, setting the tray on the bed beside her.

'Two kinds, and raisins, which you may not have seen before, Alice, and a sweet wine from Greece.' He loomed over her, long as the great bed itself, his black hair coiling back into fierce curls. He looked her up and down and cleared his throat. 'We can just eat and talk and sleep, if you wish. Become accustomed to each other.'

Was he blushing beneath his tan? *Is even he shy and uncertain?*

'You would permit this?' she murmured, startled afresh by his concern and simple kindness. She had assumed he would be eager to prove his mastery and put their marriage beyond doubt.

He knelt on the floor-strewings so their heads were level. ''tis best if we like . . . trust one another, my Alice.'

Some of the stony ice left her limbs. She leaned back against the pillows, allowing the coverlet to fall away from her naked body. She watched his eyes widen and darken and she smiled, feeling a little easier at his appreciation. Still too shy to open her arms to him, she found she could speak more naturally.

'I like the way you say that, *'my'* Alice.' She drummed her fingers on the tray. 'Can you put this on the chest for later?' *A practiced seducer would have known not to put this on the bed between us. I am glad Simon is not such.* Even so, her heartbeat stormed as a gleam entered her husband's eyes.

'Ordering me already, little nag?'

Unsure if he was teasing, but knowing he admired her hair, she flicked a long loosened tress against his wrist. Her breath stopped as Simon skimmed away the tray and sprawled onto the bed beside her.

'I know how to tame you now,' he said, and kissed her.

His scent of leather, musk and horses was familiar to her, strangely comforting, strangely arousing. She savored his hard, sinewy body, snug against hers, and how could she have suspected that his mouth would be so beguiling? With a taste of salt and sugar his lips charmed and coaxed more intimacies, nibbling hers, stroking his tongue along her sensitive bottom lip. She sighed and opened her mouth, admitting him. He explored at leisure, allowing her to do the same.

When she broke their kiss and looked at him, his eyes were as deep as a twilight sky. 'How is it you do this?' He growled. 'Yesterday you were all spines and prickles, today you are softer than petals.'

She could have said the same but, not wishing to fracture the mood between them, she closed her eyes and offered her mouth afresh.

She shivered as his fingers lightly sculptured the contours of her face. 'I thought the ladies of Constantinople with their silks and rouge were fine, but you, my English rose . . . '

She smiled, feeling truly beautiful for

the first time in her life, Simon's husky admiration healing the old wounds of her father's neglect. He rolled her out of the bed sheets and into his arms, his deep voice whispering a paean of praise.

'Lovely rose and tawny and how you glow! Like a hibiscus flower. On the battlements of Constantinople you could have stood for all women, like Helen.'

' . . . umm?' Alice mumbled, too wrapped in his embrace to greatly care.

'Helen of Troy, little nag.'

She forced her eyes wide at that. 'Unfair, my lord!'

His laughter resonated through her as he ran his thumb lightly down her spine. 'It made you look at me, though.'

She widened her eyes still more and he pinched her nose. Wondering what a hibiscus flower was like but sensing his goodwill, Alice felt bold enough to pinch him in return.

'Did you feel that?' she grumbled. Pinching Simon's hard, muscled bottom was like trying to nip iron.

'I think I should return the favor.'

Simon cupped her nether curves but he did not pinch. Dipping his long fingers over her like a potter over a sphere of clay, he molded and caressed.

Alice bit down on a queer, strangled cry that rose in her throat, fighting to remain herself when she felt to be melting into Simon, when all she wanted was more of this sweet, burning sensation that was building throughout her loins. Struggling, she tried.

'Should you not also be undressed?' she gasped.

'Not just yet.'

Simon rolled her like a curling wave onto her front. His hands stroked up and down her back, her bottom and thighs. Alice shuddered, each touch singing through her. He nuzzled the back of her neck, praising phrases in English and Greek, and his fingers spoke another, older language of touch and delight.

Wishing to do the same for him, Alice eased about, almost putting an elbow into Simon's right eye. 'Sorry!' she burst out, appalled at her own clumsiness, but he merely kissed her elbow and she was stilled and stunned — somehow her new husband had stripped. He was naked beside her and moving over her, tall and lean, with faint white scars on his chest and forearms.

Wounds all on the front, Alice thought. *My husband is a brave warrior.* 'You are handsome,' she breathed.

He laughed as if not believing her, the black curls on his head and chest shimmering like shifting sands. He cradled her face with his hands, resting his weight on his scarred forearms. 'Little wife?'

She knew what he was asking and opened her thighs beneath his, amazed at how he shivered as she traced his back and sides with her palms. 'Make us one,' she whispered.

He moved to her again, smiling as she echoed him, encouraging her to touch and taste. There was a brief, sharp moment and then closeness and pleasure, a fierce, surprising joy. She had not realized that the act of love could be so slow and tender at the start, so full and furious at the end. The sense of being one, of she and Simon worshipping each other through this blissful union, made her cry with happiness.

Contented, feeling wanted and needed for the first time in her life, Alice basked in her husband's arms and slept.

★ ★ ★

Simon came awake slowly, not quickly as he usually did. He felt adrift in a vat of pleasure, his body more alive and at the same time more relaxed than he had known it possible to be. Bedding Alice had been a revelation.

And I have slept without my nightmares of Constantinople. The city no longer burned in his mind. Alice had done that for him, too.

Grateful, he cuddled her and smiled when in sleep she jammed her toes against his shins. She was facing him and he lifted a skein of her soft, loose hair to admire her.

Her eyelashes fluttered and for an instant he hoped she would stir, that perhaps they could make love again. But no, his wife snuggled into the crook of his arm and gave a faint snore he found endearing. *I must tease her about that soon.*

The moon was high and through its bright, dusky beams, sneaking through chinks in the shutters, he saw her face. She looked perilously young in sleep, and her eyes . . .

Simon felt his heart explode into a painful, racing rhythm as he spotted the sheen of tears on her cheeks. *I am no better than the raptors of Constantinople. I have hurt her and she is too afraid to say.*

He had been proud of his ardor, of their lovemaking, but now shame shriveled him into dust. A blast of heat, then cold swept over him and he had much ado not to shudder. Feeling his eyes burning, he cradled her closer, hating himself, loathing all mankind.

I must never do this again. I cannot hurt Alice.

He gently wiped her face, images of her tears and the burning city of Constantinople flickering and superimposing before him. He knew he was not thinking sanely and he fought for breath.

I must not hurt her. I will be affectionate to her — she is so easy to care for, it will be a pleasure — and I will not cause her grief by turning aside. I never want my Alice to believe I have taken her lands and her maidenhead and no longer want her.

The thought was so painful that he scowled.

I must not hurt her in this way again. After what he had witnessed and endured overseas, he could not stand the idea. *I must keep her safe and let her see my care. I must find her sister for her, restore them to each other. Tomorrow I will rise before dawn to begin this.*

He knew he would have to be early, before Alice stirred. She tempted him enough already while she slept. Awake she would be irresistible.

And I do not want to force myself on her.

Stark awake, he did not close his eyes for the rest of that night.

6

Alice stretched and rolled onto her elbows, relaxed and content. Was the sun truly so brilliant? She glanced about the bedchamber, her heart quickening each time she spotted something of Simon's. Stretching again, she reached down for one of his socks that had slipped off the clothes chest onto the floor and recovered it, brushing it against her cheek.

Foolish, she thought, and stuffed the sock under her pillow, glad no one had witnessed her action. Where was everyone? More particularly, where was Simon?

The door opened and in he came, dressed and combed. He even wore fresh socks, so she could not tease him about that. And did she want to?

'Good morning, my heart,' he said, smiling at her as if she was a second sun. 'These are for you.' He raised his hands and for the first time she saw his gifts, an armful of presents, and such presents —

'Books!' Alice was too excited to be shy. Stripping off the sheets, she pounced upon the bestiary he had set down on the bed, her breath stopping as she opened it and found herself face to face with a lion.

'I hoped you would like them.' Simon beamed down at her.

'I do!' Delighted, she patted the pillow beside hers, thrilled anew as Simon knelt down at once and kissed her.

'I have a better gift still,' he said, stroking her hair. 'News of your sister.'

Henrietta. *I had actually forgotten her.* Blushing, Alice pushed away the gold and leather volumes and nodded without looking at her husband.

'Alexios had word come to him very early this morning,' Simon paused, his breath quickening. Glancing up at him, seeing his heightened color and busy stare, Alice remembered that she was still naked. Hastily she sat up and wound a sheet over her shoulder, shrouding herself.

'Go on, Simon, please.'

He swallowed, but gamely continued. 'Alexios is from a sailing family. He knows crews and men from all round the inner sea and beyond, including Venice and London. I told him about the mysterious Edward and Bohemond de Lyonesse and asked him to put word out to his contacts, promising money for information.'

He did this without consulting with me. Alice knew she was possibly being petty but she did not like it. Striving to keep her temper and not be a nag, little or otherwise, she said, 'He has news, already? Do your men have wings, my lord?'

'Not wings, merely good horses.' Simon chuckled and looked pleased with himself, the years seeming to drop away from him. 'It may be nothing, only rumor, but one of his cousins believes he saw Bohemond in London, in the vintner's docks close to London Bridge.'

Simon must have guessed her next question, for he raised a hand, his blue eyes twinkling. 'Bohemond was recognized by his sword and dagger. Both have distinctive pommels with his family shield emblazoned upon them.'

'So we go to London?'

Her husband shook his head. 'You must stay here. Keep safe and tend your people — '

'I know my sister,' she interrupted. Desperate to convince, desperate not to be left behind, as she so often was by her father, Alice launched herself at Simon. 'I have to come!'

'Hey!' He gathered her in and settled her on his lap, trying to kiss her, but she turned her head.

'Let me speak,' she gasped. 'Do you not understand why I have to come with you? Henrietta does not know you. She may not even know our father is dead.'

'Or perhaps Bohemond and Edward already know and are making plans accordingly.'

'And if they do and they arrive here while you are absent? If Edward claims my sister's lands as her betrothed? How do I stop them?'

Simon scowled. 'I will leave you well-guarded.'

'Safer still with you, my lord,' said Alice cunningly.

* * *

She had him, Simon thought, rubbing the back of his neck with an anxious hand. Having her perched naked on his knees was turning out to be a huge mistake — Alice might not guess the depth of his distraction, but in truth he could scarcely reason. The feel of her trusting, pliant body, the sweet scent of her hair, her hopeful, questing look and rosy smile, all delivered hammer blows to his plan to remain affectionate but chaste. He longed to tip her into bed again and spend the day with her there.

But he had vowed not to hurt her more, and he had sworn to find her sister. *Why can she not come with me? She wants to go, you want to take her.* 'We cannot travel in state,' he said, unsure why he was still trying to argue against their own wishes. 'The search may take us to low places and dismal streets. As a lady you will be too conspicuous, too tempting a target.'

You are already, though you do not know it. He had given her the books as a token of his respect for her and because he had treasured them. Yet, valuable as these works of gold and vellum were, Alice was more. She was priceless.

Thunderstruck by this revelation, he watched his beguiling new wife drape her loosened hair across her breasts, possibly an unconscious gesture of what she had in mind. 'So I go with you as a maid and leave Beatrix here. I know you can protect me.'

Her sweet confidence at once reminded him of those women he had not been able to save within the burning, sacked city of Constantinople. 'No,' he choked, the stench of death and burning rising in his nostrils afresh.

His face or body must have betrayed him, for fearlessly she clasped his hand and gently kissed his shoulder. 'London is not Constantinople,' she said quietly. 'It has thieves and ruffians, yes, but it is not under siege. My father visited many times.'

'And was set upon by scoundrels,' Simon reminded her.

'Whom you drove away,' she reminded him in return. 'Once only, when he was old and sickening. I will heed all your warnings, Simon, obey all your instructions. Only let me come, for my sister's sake.'

He said nothing. The feel of her hand around his was strangely comforting, returning him to himself, to this room in England — *with my Alice.*

Just as he would have embraced her,

she pitched off him, whirling the sheet about herself. 'Let me find suitable clothes and you shall see,' she promised, then sped to the door, opened it a crack and called for Beatrix.

7

After three days of hard riding they were in Westminster, beside the city of London. In her maid's disguise of a faded scarlet gown and earth-colored hooded head-rail, Alice looked out from the upper window of the Rose Inn, where Simon had found them a room. She was so weary and aching that she longed to sleep but, once Simon had gone out into the city with Alexios to seek further news of her sister, sleep became impossible.

But I am here, with Simon.

She had ridden alongside him on one of his black horses and slept each night in his arms, too stunned by the relentless travel to do more than take a few mouthfuls of pottage and a hasty drink, then lie down. Simon had never scolded her, as she feared he might, ashamed that he might consider her a weakling. He called her a good journeywoman and a pretty maid.

At night he had kissed and cuddled her, but no more than that. Exhausted as she was, she was glad to rest even though mornings found her with a headache, backache and doddery legs.

But now, when he had found her a room and a comfortable bed, she paced the sloping-roofed chamber, listening to the guards posted outside and the roar of London down the river.

Has he found Henrietta? Please God, let it be so.

She hit the roof with her fist once in frustration, once in hope, then whipped about to the window. Opening the shutters she leaned out, fighting not to gag at the sheer city stink. The river beyond was a bright silver ribbon, full of little boats and yelling oarsmen. Walking away from its shelving banks, directly beneath the jetty of the Rose Inn, came a familiar tall, dark figure, striding swiftly over the refuse-strewn cobbles.

Amazingly, Simon knew she watched

for him. He raised his head and waved, mouthing, 'More news.'

She waved back then flew to the door, pushing it open and finding it jammed after less than a finger's width. Desperate to see Simon, to hear his news, she hammered on the timbers.

'Hey, hey, I am coming.' The door creaked back and her husband swept inside, catching her by the elbows. 'Why such noise?'

'You shut me in!' Behind Simon she saw his blond second, Alexios, looking surprised, and several more of his men hiding smiles. Her indignation increased. 'How would you like it if I locked you in a room and went out without word of when I would return?'

'Come.' Black-browed, Simon slammed the door on the onlookers and pulled her with him to the bed. He sat down and hauled her onto his lap.

'Quiet,' he ordered, when she was about to say more. 'You should want to hear about your sister, instead of abusing me before my men. That is why you are here, after all.'

I am not abusing anyone. Alice clamped her jaws together on the rising answer and nodded. Saving Henrietta was all that mattered.

Frowning still, Simon tipped up her chin, stared at her for a long instant, then spoke. 'A young maid answering your sister's description was seen four days ago in the household of Bohemond de Lyonesse as they attended the church of Saint Magnus, close to London Bridge.'

She lives! Alice flung her arms around Simon's neck and hugged him in sheer thankfulness and relief. 'Is she . . . ?' But it was impossible to finish her question. When Simon's arms locked about her she discovered to her shame and horror that she was weeping warm, silent tears as the dark tension she had held close-in for weeks released.

'All will be well.' Stiffly, Simon stroked her back. 'Truly, the girl is healthy and well dressed, clearly well regarded and well looked after.'

Alice nodded a second time, crying harder than ever. *He will utterly despise me and he will be right to do so.* Dimly, through her own ragged breathing, she heard Simon give a mumbled curse and felt his easy strength as he lifted her into the middle of the bed with him. They lay intertwined, he running his fingers through her hair. 'Soon she will be safe with you again, my Alice,' he whispered against her ear. 'Very soon.'

When? Alice wanted to ask but the urgent question died on her tongue. Instead, unstrung and feeling safer than she had in years, she dropped into a dreamless sleep.

Simon eased her slumbering form into the middle of the bed and padded to the door. After some quiet words with Alexios he shut the world out again and returned to his wife. By her reactions she had again confounded him. When she had blazed at him, showing him up before Alexios and the others, he had been strongly tempted to drape her over his knee and spank her.

But then she had startled him afresh by hurling herself into his arms in thankfulness. Indeed, her relief at hearing that Henrietta was safe was so profound that it had overwhelmed her.

I should have expected that. This is her younger, dearly loved sister. Keep that always in mind and show her the mercy that the women of Constantinople deserved and never received.

He felt divided within himself, that was the trouble. Alice was so slender and small he longed to wrap her in furs and feed her manchet rolls spread with butter and honey. In her simple home-spun clothes she looked to be no lady at all, merely a very pretty maid and a nicely disheveled one at that, with her hair spilling from her mud-colored cap. *A fit mate for a mercenary. For sure she does well for me.* Watching her sleep, her lashes trembling against her pale cheeks, her hair all tangled, he experienced a still deeper surge of protectiveness, bewildering in its intensity. At the same time he recalled her bright fury and wanted to clash with her again.

He drew her into his arms, gently cupping her backside for his own pleasure. Even in sleep she sighed, responding to him. *But I must not hurt her again.* Regretfully, he withdrew his hand, stroking her back instead. The caress tormented him afresh, made his blood sing in his ears, but he did not care. It comforted Alice and he felt more alive than he had for months. Reveling in her scent and softness, he closed his eyes.

★　★　★

She was trapped in shackles of iron. Alice squirmed and the shackles tightened more, white hot about her breasts and thighs. She yelped, waking fully, and found herself captured by Simon. He was moaning and twitching in his sleep.

'You hurt me,' she murmured urgently against his neck. 'Simon!' She could not free her arms to give him a shake so she leaned up and nipped his ear. Still he did not let her go, clamping her closer.

'Must protect — ' he ground out, through clenched teeth. 'Keep safe . . . God forgive me! I could do naught for the others . . . '

He talks in his sleep of Constantinople, of the sacking of the city. Even when she had been mewed up in the English countryside, Alice had heard of the fall of Constantinople. She could not begin to imagine the horrors Simon had witnessed but she had to help him.

She relaxed in his arms and began to sing quietly, a little lullaby she remembered Euphemia singing to her. She felt the tension seeping away from Simon's long limbs and sang on, hoping she was doing right.

'No!' He shouted and came awake.

'Tell me.' Alice gripped his hands, determined to keep him with her as his men knocked on the door.

'All is well,' Simon called out and a heavy, anxious silence replaced the knocking. He shook himself like a great bear but Alice pinned him to the bed with an arm and leg.

'Tell me,' she said again.

He glanced at her attempt to keep him still, amusement sparking in his blue eyes. 'I know we are husband and wife but we should not lie all day abed, my Alice.'

'You were dreaming. Tell me what you saw,' she persisted.

For an instant she thought he would sweep her aside, or tickle her, but then he rolled onto his stomach, jamming his fists under his chin as if he were years younger. 'Why do you want such stuff in your head?' he growled, his black brows drawn together in solid line across his forehead.

'So I may understand.' She did not say that the telling might ease his memories, she did not know if that was true. 'What happened?'

He sighed and said quickly, 'I dream of Constantinople burning, many dreams, often the same ones. This is the worst. There was a woman, trapped in one of the houses. I tried to reach her, to drag her through her window onto the tower where I had my men. She held out her arms to me.'

His breath stopped and he closed his eyes. 'The floor beneath her was burning and it fell through, taking her with it. I heard her scream and saw her face as she fell. I grabbed for her but could not catch her. I could not save her.'

He opened his eyes and glared at her. 'I have confessed this to no one. There were others, too. I witnessed women and girls violated as Constantinople fell. I could do nothing to save them, do you understand? Such was the close press of fighting between me and those poor creatures, I could not help them. I could not even reach them! I live with that knowledge because I must. Do you really want to hear of them?'

'Yes,' said Alice simply, determined not to flinch away. 'I want to know it all.' *If I know what haunts him I can help him*. A tiny, unworthy part of her relished the fact that he had told no one else. An even worse part hissed the question, *was the woman who fell beautiful?*

'Sir?' Alexios scratched at the door again.

'They will think we have made love,' Alice said softly, astonishing herself with her boldness. *But why not tease Simon a little? If he scolds me for being saucy, he does not think then of burning women, or of violated girls.* A deeper, secret part of her wanted him to make it true, for them to join together and be one. *It would not heal him, for some memories are beyond healing, but it would be a comfort. And now I understand why he is wary. Big as he is and small as I am, he will not want to force me.*

Her husband snorted. 'I hope I take longer than that in the art of loving.' He smacked her on her bottom and rolled off the mattress. 'Up wife, we have plans to make.'

Plans to rescue Henrietta. And I will be part of them. 'Yes, husband,' she said, smiling at the thought. Enjoying the warm heat in her rump, she rose with him and began to reorder her hair.

Find my sister and seduce my husband. Two very pleasant tasks.

8

'I must go with you,' Alice argued, itching to jab Simon in his flat stomach to silence his protests. As Alexios frowned and pinched the top of his long nose with his elegant fingers, Alice knew that even Simon's second considered her reasons to join them the merest froth.

She turned to the window and looked out, seeing the wife of the innkeeper hurrying back from a quayside market, carrying a great fish in a pail. What did that woman think of her being shut in this chamber with all these men? Feeling herself blush again and avoiding a glance at the bed, Alice was still determined to speak. 'I am the only one of you who knows Henrietta.'

As handsome as a gold and silver statue come to life, Alexios was eager to suggest a compromise. 'My lady, I draw well. If you describe your sister I will fashion a likeness of her that we may show about. It will also be a reminder for us.'

Alice shook her head. 'I know my sister best. Think of this, too — I will not be fastened in this room while others search. If need be, I will climb out of the window.'

'My lady!' If a statue could look indignant, it would wear the same expression as Alexios did.

'Enough.' Simon's deep voice cut across them both. 'Now, we may have found the lady. We should make haste to recover her. A small scouting party is best for this. Alice and I shall walk out into the streets near London Bridge to discover what we may. Alexios, you and the others scour the river and the docks, question the boatmen and rowers. We meet here again at sunset.'

In truth, little time had passed since Simon had returned to the Rose Inn with his wondrous news, but Alice was glad to fall in with his plan. 'I agree.'

As Simon looked her up and down she wondered for a moment if she had gone too far, but he said merely, 'The day is warm. You will not need a cloak. Stay close to me.' He took her hand in a grip of steel, and as they all clattered down the inn stairs and out into the street he did not release her.

Down at ground level Alice almost tripped several times in the cart ruts and stinking mud of London, but Simon strode along, hustling her with him. She almost protested but knew he would merely say that she had wanted to come.

'Mistress!' She caught the eye of a flower-seller standing a sword's length away from them on the junction of two alleyways. Simon was forced to stop as the woman and her children blocked the alleyway ahead of him with their buckets of fresh violets, iris and roses. She felt his grip tighten on her fingers.

'Flowers for your sister?' he asked.

'Against the foul smells and disease, my lord,' she replied, as the flower-seller launched into a praise of Simon's looks and breeding and what flowers would suit him.

'A posy of violets for my defiant girl, if you please,' Simon told the flower-seller, and then he turned back to her. Before she knew what he was about to do, he caught her by her skirts and tugged her close murmuring, 'Though I like you in apple blossom better.'

He is going to kiss me out here in the street! To avoid his lowering head, Alice said quickly, 'Defiant, my lord? How so? I cannot keep pace with you if we go so fast that I fall and break my leg.'

His eyes narrowed. The flower seller deftly palmed the coin he tossed and retreated in a whiff of violets and lavender. Simon loomed an instant longer then pounced. The posy of violets was crushed between them as he wound her into his arms and his mouth smothered her protest.

'Henrietta,' she whispered, when she could speak, but he deepened their embrace and she forgot all words. Heat and pleasure sparkled through her as he kissed her again and again.

'Maddening wench.'

He caressed her bottom through her skirts, his touch intimate, but not intimate enough. *Please*, she thought, but did not know if she was pleading for him to stop or to go on. He swung her lightly against the timbered wall of the house, her rump pressed against the warm wood as his strong hands encircled her waist. A passing apprentice laughed and made a lewd jest but his words were no more than a bubble. She was floating, caught between desire and a dream.

'We should move,' Simon said but he did not stir. Alice, uncaring now if anyone could see them or not, put her arms around his neck. Simon's starkly handsome face filled her world and then she could see only his eyes, as blue as twilight.

'Lovely, naughty nag.' His eyes smiled at her. His lips brushed her forehead, cheek and mouth.

'Your maid, sir.' She tried to bob him a swift curtsey but could not move from his embrace.

'My maid.'

She sighed into his kiss. The hour of the day, the passing carters and sellers, the distant sound of church bells, these had no meaning to her. From the corner of her half-closed eyes she saw the posy of violets he had bought her, trapped in his belt buckle. She tugged at the posy and he chuckled and leaned close again, grasping her hand. 'Not yet,' he said, nipping her lower lip with his teeth.

Simon wanted to toss her over his shoulder and hurry to the nearest stew to have his way with her. Or take her here in the street, against the house wall, battering into her pliant, yielding body. *Mother of Christ, I am as bad as the crusaders who sacked Constantinople.* But Alice seemed as eager as he was. Her glowing skin was smoother than a pearl and she trembled with delight in his embrace. Kissing her had become a glimpse of heaven. She tasted sweet, sweetly trusting and passionate, all together.

Abruptly, her eyes widened and she stiffened in his arms, breaking free the instant he relaxed his hold. A tall stately blonde, closely escorted by four men-at-arms, strolled past the junction of the alleyway.

'Henrietta!' Alice shouted. The young woman turned, passed over Alice in a single glance and stared at Simon. She called out a command in Norman French. Two of her escorts drew their swords and approached.

'It is me, beloved . . . sister!' Still Alice was trying to convince the haughty blonde, but Simon realized that the young woman was not listening. He plucked Alice out of the path of those glittering blades and stalked into the middle of the street.

'There is still time for you to walk away,' he told the pair.

They rushed him, slashing and cutting clumsily, yelling to give each other courage. Dangerous fools, in fact, and he whipped past their attacks, slammed his boot into the backside of one and kicked him into the other. *A mercenary* uses *any weapon, including his feet*. Down they went in a swirl of color and noise into the mud and he snatched up a hurdle, ripped it from the soft earth and threw it on top of them.

'Hey!' yelled a householder as his pig escaped through the gap the missing hurdle had made.

Simon left the pig, householder, and men struggling and jogged back to Alice. His brief skirmish had been almost comic, but her face was as pale as milk. 'She set those men on us, on me,' she said.

She swayed and he feared she might faint but then, before he could stop her, she straightened and ran along the alley, away from his increasingly filthy would-be assailants and toward the tall blonde. Cursing, Simon chased after her.

He caught up with Alice and they reached the junction together. The young woman and her remaining escorts were gone.

9

Somehow Alice forced her clammy limbs to move again and she turned to her panting companion. Simon watched her, pity scored into his face. Yet why should he be sorry? 'We should return to the Rose.' Her mouth felt to be working and her voice sounded normal. 'We must talk.'

Back along the street, she allowed Simon to nudge her gently away from a steaming pile of dung she would have toiled through unnoticing. She let him stalk ahead to the inn, calling for mulled wine and food to be brought to their room. Once inside she lay back on the bed and felt him remove her shoes.

He drew a coverlet over her and knelt so their eyes were level. 'If that were truly your sister, that is good. We know she is safe and we know where she is. I saw the badges of the men and we may track them. Next time you will be dressed in your finest and Henrietta will know you.'

'Yes.' What else was there to say?

She heard a timid knock at the door and a maid entered with their wine and food. Simon poured her a cup, offered it as if she was a great lady in a grand household, not a failed sister close to weeping and hiding in bed.

'Did you see the maid?' he asked, as she took the warm cup.

Alice nodded, sitting upright. Simon at once piled pillows about her. 'I am not yet with child,' she snapped, then felt ashamed of her own misery and pettishness. 'Forgive me.'

'No matter. Was the maid a redhead?'

'What?' She understood what he was about and scowled. 'I did not notice, but that is different! That is a maid. I am Henrietta's sister.'

'You have not seen each other for months. And I doubt if she has ever seen you in a common gown. As you say yourself, my Alice, she will not have noticed you, a mere maid.'

'I did not say mere.'

'Does your sister know that your father is dead?'

Alice hated these questions, hated her husband's cool logic. 'You have asked before and my answer is the same. I do not know.'

Simon poured himself a cup of wine. 'Would you prefer to be alone?'

When she did not answer he drained his cup and walked to the closed door. He put his hand on the latch. 'Mark this,' he said, without turning. 'We do not know what Bohemond and Edward may have told your sister. She may not have been acting against you but against me, a stranger.'

'It is not all about you.'

She expected him to leave but instead he kicked the door and spun back. In three strides he flung himself beside her, bouncing the mattress so much that she spilled part of the wine on her hand.

'Ow!' She sucked at the burning

liquid but Simon was leaning over her, his face suddenly concerned.

'Let me see, sweetheart.'

The endearment, his patience and consideration in the teeth of her foul mood, wrung fresh tears from her. 'She did not know me!' she cried, while Simon gathered her to him and rocked her.

'She did not see you. Hush now! Nothing is impossible. We shall make a plan and save her.'

'She does not wish to be saved,' Alice grumbled against his shoulder.

'She is fourteen and needs saving. Have some more wine, yes? You need warming up.'

Simon chafed her chilled hands, relieved that the wine had not burned her and glad when the milky paleness began to seep away from her narrow little face. His wife's taut, cold answers, her stiffness and her resentment toward him had worried rather than angered him, which was why he had been determined not to leave her. *She scratches at me but what of it?* Even when he had kicked the door in the teeth of one of her particularly curt replies he had understood. She had endured a bitter shock. He was not such a petty tyrant that he would scold her for lashing out in return — he knew only too well how that worked. Now he was glad she was in his arms again, and without a quarrel first.

Her sister is a fool, but she is but fourteen years old. How wise were you at fourteen? What has that bastard de Lyonesse told her, if anything?

He coaxed Alice to sip the mulled wine, taking a drink himself.

'Henrietta must be lodged close,' Alice said suddenly. 'She vanished off the street quicker than a morning mist.'

'I agree,' said Simon, proud of her reasoning. He was less pleased when she sat up straight against the pillows and burst out, 'What if they decide to move elsewhere or leave London?'

'They will not.' He crossed his fingers.

'But if they do?'

'A man like Bohemond travels in state. We shall find them on the road.' Deciding that she would no more stay in bed and relax than an icicle would stay cold at midsummer, Simon poured two more cups of wine and passed her a small curd tart. 'Eat up. We should go out again.'

'Where?'

He smiled. She looked young again and pretty, the zest of hope granting her energy. Her excitement was engaging. 'What does your sister enjoy? When she was at home with you, how did she pass her time?'

'In the stables or out on the meadows,' replied Alice at once. 'She once told me that if she could have chosen to be born as whatever she wished, she would have been a horse, or a messenger, riding everywhere.' Her green eyes glowed as she hugged her knees. 'Oh, Simon, you are right! That is a way to find her, in the pasture lands around here!'

If Edward allows her to visit such places. Simon said nothing. If he and his wife were not to spend the time languid in bed then they were best up and active. And he liked her hopeful, ardent look, he liked to see her smiling and happy.

'Eat up, then,' he said, finding her shoes beneath the bed and handing them to her. 'I shall leave a message with the innkeeper so Alexios knows where we are. I shall buy you another posy, too, seeing as you lost the first.'

'No, you did,' Alice answered instantly, with her accustomed fire, and then she frowned. 'Simon, you do not need to buy me anything.'

'Maybe not, but I want to.'

And we shall walk to the horse pastures, not ride, so we have more time together.

* * *

He kept his promise. Alice lowered her head and inhaled the sweet-smelling violets and lavender, the scent making her briefly lightheaded. Simon had bought her three posies from three different sellers. Walking beside him, arm in arm, she wished she could be more appreciative.

Had I not seen Henrietta, this day would have been good for me. I thank God she is alive and well and wish I could feel more than that. Her sister could not have recognized her, could she? *Or does she believe I betrayed her in some way?*

The idea was so terrible she shied away from it, leaning against her husband for comfort. Again, Simon had surprised her, kept surprising her. He had been willing to bring her to London and willing to share some of his darker past with her. So far, he was proving much more than the bully and braggart she had feared he might be. His tanned, handsome face was often unreadable but strangely he was not. She liked him and to her delight she realized he liked her.

Pray God we shall continue to do well together. But I must remember to show him I want him, to show that I welcome his attentions, or he will think I am like the poor women of Constantinople and never come near me.

It was a sadness to her that he should be so haunted. *And I was worried he had married me solely for my lands . . .*

She patted his arm and he grinned at her. As she looked up into his smiling blue eyes, Henrietta's unkindness lifted a little more from her spirits. 'Do you like the city?' she asked.

'I like the river and the gardens,' he answered. 'The houses seem low and drab to me. There were many buildings of marble and gold in Constantinople.'

'And no hibiscus flowers here.'

'Ah, you remembered!'

She smiled, pleased that he was pleased. 'You also compared me to Helen of Troy.' *He saved you in the street, too, when Henrietta set those brutes on you.* Trying to forget what her sister had done, she found herself remembering Simon's speed and easy grace in the fight, his tautened muscles and long, lean legs. Smiling at the memory she pointed to distant London Bridge, its ramshackle shops and jetties casting black shadows on the water. 'Were there bridges like that one in Constantinople?'

He chuckled, the idea clearly absurd. 'Shall we go? If we are to walk to the bridge, cross it and return to the Rose Inn before curfew, we should hasten a little.'

She thought of the press of people sweating in the narrow streets and jostling over the bridge and considered their being set upon earlier. *What if we should be attacked again? I do not want Simon hurt because of me.* 'We will see more of the water meadows and pastures from the river,' she said, realizing as she spoke that it was true. 'Can we not take a boat? It would be faster.'

For an instant she thought his eyes clouded in disappointment and then he nodded. 'Aye, you are right, my Alice. Come, then.'

* * *

He wanted their boat trip to last for longer than it did but when the ferry docked beside the palace of Lambeth he ignored the stares of the German and French merchants and offered Alice his arm.

After a hesitation she took it and they disembarked. 'They think I am a servant girl, overreaching her place,' she murmured, as they passed a red-cheeked trader on the key side, sweating in his expensive, hot furs. 'What would you do with me if I were?'

His spirits rose at her blatant invitation to play. 'A kiss, to start with.' He made good his threat, amused and flattered afresh when she stood on tiptoes and then even on top of his boots to return his embrace.

'We are not in a bathhouse now,' he murmured, savoring the feel of her back and her tiny waist.

Her green eyes twinkled. 'Ah, you remembered!' she said, in an echo of his earlier speech, a rosy blush flooding her face as his fingers lightly played over her body, but she did not attempt to break free. 'What next, sir?'

Abruptly, unwelcomingly, Simon sensed that they were being watched by other, more dangerous onlookers than the outraged traders. He brought Alice within the shield of his arm and gripped his sword, scanning the fields beyond the palace and the lepers' hospital before searching nearer for the impending threat.

'My lord Simon!' To his astonishment — and yes, annoyance for being interrupted when he had hoped to have Alice to himself — Alexios cantered from the shade of the palace buildings and drew rein beside them.

'Sir, we have tracked the girl here!'

Simon raised his eyebrows and his second hastily amended.

'The Lady Henrietta, I mean, by your leave. She rides on a bay palfrey, over there beyond the chestnut trees.'

'It may not be her,' he warned Alice, who had instantly stiffened like a hound on a scent, but through the heat haze and dust of exercising horses he spotted a slender female rider with a cool, familiar look and a shimmer of yellow hair. Two squires rode alongside her. They were armed with clubs.

'Gold frees tongues and buys news everywhere.' Alice squinted into the haze. 'But where is Edward?'

Alexios answered her. 'The King is due for Westminster today, 'tis said. Edward will have gone to the royal hall to seek audience with King John and to plead his case to marry your sister.'

Simon allowed Alice to break free of his embrace and watched as she stepped forward, looking ready to chase after the bay palfrey and its rider.

'Then why not take her with him?' she asked.

'He may not trust the king,' said Simon. 'Your father told me that King John likes to acquire heiresses and keep them close by him on his royal progress. Keep them as near prisoners, in fact.'

At the mention of Henry Martinswood Alice bowed her head, her lips moving as if in prayer. When she looked up at him again her mood had changed. She looked determined and excited together.

'Can you divert her guards so I may talk to her?'

'But your dress, my lady,' Alexios began, falling silent at once as Alice raised a hand. Her face was solemn, almost regal, very different from the teasing little maid who had kissed him so ardently moments earlier. Again, Simon felt proud of her. *She is such a woman, my wife.*

'This time Henrietta will see me,' she said, 'and she will listen.'

10

Henrietta yawned behind her glove and willed the hours to pass. Edward had begged her to marry him and she had agreed, but since then her days had grown dull. Bohemond was no longer amusing and snapped at her. Edward, his handsome face marred by a frown, said she must be patient and wait. At dinner he drummed his fingers on the table, just as her father did. It was all very disappointing.

Henrietta sighed again. Over the past few days she had realized that Edward's hair was thinning and that his breath smelled. Had she not had Beauty to ride she might have been tempted to run away again, this time to a nunnery.

I miss Alice. She could always make me laugh.

The court of Queen Eleanor had been dull. The lady had been old and no longer interested in courts of love. Henrietta was bored while serving there until Edward and Bohemond appeared and Edward had courted her with songs and gifts. When the old queen had died that spring, Henrietta had been happy to leave with him. *He does not sing to me now. He is always rushing off, seeking something, trying to find the king.* She had told him that King John would agree to their marriage. Why should he not? They were both loyal.

Behind her she heard shouting, a challenge. The apprentices here were quarrelsome and she took no notice. She also ignored her squires and their overanxious pleas, 'Beware, my lady! Stay close!'

She spurred Beauty and cantered closer to the river, toward the chestnut trees. A woman had picked some of the chestnuts' flower spikes and was swaying with them, to and fro, in a jerky, awkward manner. Henrietta snorted and prepared to ride on.

'Do you remember how you wanted

to be a dancer?'

The woman, a mere maid, called out to her as if she were an equal and once she had started, she did not stop. 'Before that you wished to be a scholar, before that an abbess . . . '

Henrietta narrowed her eyes and glanced around for her two escorts but they were yards behind, swinging their clubs at a tall, dark-haired man whom she realized was very good-looking, in a dangerous kind of way. As she stared, wondering who the stranger was and thinking that she would certainly tell Edward how his squires had neglected her, the dark-haired man nimbly avoided their weapons.

But now, just at the climax of the fight, the wretched maid shouted at her again.

'Your eyes used to be better than this, Henrietta! Has your time in France weakened them? Look at me! See me, not my clothes!'

'She is a spoiled and sinful child,' drawled a new, masculine voice.

Henrietta gasped as a stranger as blond as a Viking and as handsome as a pagan god stepped between her and the maid. Behind her she heard more yelling. Twisting round in the saddle, she saw the dark-haired giant wrest a stave from one of the squires and brandish it at the second.

'Do not hurt them!' cried the maid, astonishingly running toward rather than away from the skirmish.

'Henrietta,' said the handsome stranger, standing in front of Beauty with his arms folded across his mighty chest, 'Do you not know your own sister? Are you so blind, so ungrateful? My lady Alice has been seeking you for weeks and you sit up there on your pretty horse without a care for her suffering. How can you do it?'

Flinching at his scorn, Henrietta looked again with more care, looked at the maid and the clumsy, careless way she ran over her own skirts and understood.

'Alice.' Her voice was no more than a whisper. *My sister, here? And the old man, is he here, too?*

'I will help you down.' The handsome stranger was at her stirrup, reaching up for her. In a too-brief moment she was in his arms and then set down lightly on the grass. His eyes were gray, like a winter sea. He was very strong. She wet her dry lips with her tongue. 'Your name, sir?'

'Alexios of Constantinople, and now London.' He did not bow but he smiled and that was enough of a wonder. 'Come. I will take you to your sister.'

Dazzled, Henrietta complied.

11

With his wife, her sister, and the rest of his troop safely returned to the Rose Inn, Simon silently thanked God for his second in command. Alexios had instantly taken Henrietta in hand, ordering her firmly but kindly, like an older brother. Thus far, the young woman had responded without a single complaint.

Right now Henrietta and Alice were with Alexios in the stables, setting guards on Henrietta's palfrey and bedding Beauty and their other horses down for the night.

Simon had ordered food for them all and brought to them inside the chamber when Alice entered. She crossed to the window and opened the shutters wide, looking toward the river.

He joined her at the window. He would have preferred to join her in bed, but tonight she and Henrietta would be sharing that and he would be sleeping outside, on the landing with his men. 'Your sister?'

'Still with her horse. Alexios is with her.' Grimacing as she did so, Alice twisted her head this way and that. Simon came behind her and began to knead the tight muscles at the back of her neck.

'She knows about Father now.' With a sigh, Alice turned into the crook of his arm, her head dropping as he continued to massage her shoulders. He said nothing, sensing there was more and, indeed, after a moment, Alice added, 'She knows he is dead but she talks of nothing but Alexios. Everything is Alexios. Even Edward seems forgotten.'

'Fourteen is a changeable age,' Simon remarked, switching hands to palm down her spine. 'A heartless age.' *Why indeed should she care for Henry Martinswood, who cast her off? If I know anything of Alice, my warm-hearted wife will not have told Henrietta that their father disinherited her before he died, but the girl would still have sensed his indifference.* 'Even little children know when they are not loved,' he said aloud. 'And with your father being as he was . . . '

Recalling Henry's stubbornness, Simon also wondered if Henrietta shared that trait with her father, especially when crossed.

Henrietta may be willful, but she is beautiful. Alice is right about that. Seen this close up, Alice's sister had the kind of beauty that stopped the talk in rooms or among passersby on the street. Clearly the girl was accustomed to attention, to being indulged because of her golden beauty and to having her own way.

'She told me that she and Edward have not shared a bed,' Alice yawned and began a half-hearted rub of his back. 'He was waiting for marriage.'

Tactfully, Simon said only: 'Alexios will look after her. She will be safe with him.'

Alice looked up at him with a half-smile, her hand resting on his shoulder. 'He orders her about a good deal.'

'Does she object?'

'No.' Alice sighed again. 'And they make a fine pair. They are both as blonde and handsome as each other.'

Simon smiled. 'I prefer brunettes.'

'And I dark-haired men.' Alice yawned a second time and snuggled closer. 'I wish we were home now.'

'We can leave tomorrow.'

She leaned back a little in his arms and shook her head. 'But the king and his list of heiresses?'

Simon smiled and brushed her cheek with his fingers. 'How do we know if you and Henrietta are even on that list? We only have Bohemond de Lyonesse's word. I say we go home.'

He waited and sure enough she picked him up. 'You say, husband?'

Husband. He smiled at the proprietorial way she used the word. 'Do you object, my Alice? You can teach me how to prune apple trees and to pick berries.'

'You do not prune apples at this time of year,' came her cheeky reply, and he was content. *Let her think of her garden. Let Alexios continue to beguile her sister. Tomorrow we shall go home.*

★ ★ ★

Tonight she intended to seduce him. How she would do that when she was in one room and he was not, she refused to worry about. *Henrietta sleeps like a well-fed baby once she is asleep. I will slip out of our chamber then.*

Alice forced herself to eat a little of the oyster and venison pies that Simon had bought for all of them. Sitting on the bed with her sister, she drank several cups of the wine, careful not to catch her husband's eye in case she gave away her loving plan. They retired early and she was glad, deciding she would be even happier if her sister abruptly fell asleep in the midst of comparing Alexios and Edward — to Alexios's advantage, no doubt.

Meanwhile, the instant the door closed on Simon's broad, retreating back, Henrietta flung herself backward with such force that Alice was afraid her sister would burst the straw mattress. 'Careful!' she warned, telling herself at the same time that it would not do for her to be so vigorous and abandoned with Simon. *I want to beguile him, not bounce him out of our bed.*

Jerking bolt upright again, Henrietta tossed off one of Alexios's favorite oaths. 'Blessed Mother of God, you sound like Father! He always ordered me about and complained.' Her pretty mouth wobbled into a sulky downward pout. 'Why did he do that? Why did he never . . . care?'

For an icy, panicked instant, Alice wondered if Henrietta had somehow learned that their father had cast her off before he died. Then she recalled Simon's steady voice and his calm words, *Children know when they are not loved.* That was bad enough, but at least her sister had not known of Henry Martinswood's final cruelty, and would never do so. *No, I shall never tell her.*

'You are mistaken, beloved,' she answered,

as her heartbeat grew steadier and she plumbed her memory for any pleasant recollection of their dead, unmissed parent. She brought up nothing, only a scowling face and carping voice. 'He loved you, Herri,' she added weakly, praying her sister would not demand proof.

Henrietta allowed her childish nickname to pass without comment and shrugged. Her golden plaits flashed and dazzled in the bedside candle flame as she shook her head. 'He never let us go anywhere or do anything,' she complained, cool again.

'That is true for all fathers everywhere,' Alice said quietly, and she took out a comb so she could offer to reorder her sister's lush hair. 'Did Alexios tell you of the ladies in Constantinople, who are kept inside and closely guarded?'

'Of course. Alexios and I share everything.' Following an old habit of theirs, Henrietta turned and knelt up on the mattress so that Alice could undo her plaits. 'He has amazing gray eyes, you know.'

I like blue eyes. Alice combed and combed until Henrietta's hair crackled. Her sister sighed, relaxing under her gentle ministrations, and Alice wished she could offer more comfort. 'Our father did his best,' she said softly.

'He did allow me to go to France,' Henrietta conceded. In another quicksilver change of mood she ripped her head round, scarcely flinching as the comb caught in her glittering tresses, and cast herself into Alice's arms, rocking them both with the force of her embrace. 'But I wish you could have come, too.'

There was a burning behind Alice's eyes and what felt to be a smoldering brand stuck in her throat.

'Sorry for setting the men on you in the street,' Henrietta whispered. 'That was wrong, I know.'

Determined not to cry, Alice tightened her arms around her sister. 'No matter. That is past, forgotten.' *Forgiven. I no longer care what she did then, or for why.* 'I have missed you so much, little one.'

'I am taller and prettier than you are,' Henrietta sniffed, a red-nosed Helen of Troy. 'But you have father's eyes.' She leaned back a little and looked closely at Alice. 'Yes. His eyes, but kind.' Changeable as only a fourteen-year-old can be, she calmly kissed Alice's cheek. 'I am most glad to see you. I like your Simon, though he scared me at first.'

Taking advantage of Alice's astonished silence, Henrietta lifted the comb from her hair. 'Turn about and let me loose and dress your hair. I know a cunning new style with many pins. Alexios told me of it and I know Simon will adore it.'

* * *

It was perhaps an hour later. Tucked up in the covers, looking puppy-soft and relaxed, Henrietta had indeed tumbled into sleep in the middle of a rambling story of Alexios's boyhood. Listening to her soft breathing. Alice eased herself out of bed, pausing a moment to look back at her sleeping younger sister.

Thank God she will never know that our father disowned her. Thank God she is safe.

A shudder overcame her as her thoughts stuck on what so easily might have happened, the tens — no, hundreds — of ghastly things that might have befallen her. *This kind of horror is real for Simon. I must ensure he endures it as little as possible. Henrietta is safe and I will keep her safe, and as for my husband —*

Now. It must be now.

With trembling fingers she pulled on her maid's clothes and sped from the bed to the door. She put her face to the smooth planks and heard snoring beyond, no talking. She smiled and softly unlatched the lock.

The landing was darker than the bedchamber and the knots of men, rolled in their cloaks, looked like tree roots. Praying she would not be clumsy this one time and tread on any, she crept forward, inching each step.

A sinewy arm wound about her waist, a large hand gently covered her mouth.

'I was coming to find you,' Simon whispered against her neck. Then he lifted her into his arms and bore her away. 'I know a place.'

Moving more quietly than she could, he walked out of the Rose Inn with her and away from the river. She thought of mentioning cut-purses or spies but no one troubled them. *No one dare attack my mercenary, my champion*, she thought proudly, feeling his easy strength as he strolled through the empty streets with her. The moon was high and bright and the alleyways quiet. In a dim garden a chicken clucked as they passed, and later a dog yapped, but soon they were in meadows, with tall grasses and flowers around them.

'You can put me down,' Alice said, as the feathery heads of grass tickled her legs. In the moonlight she could see a rising spire of a church with scaffolding round it.

'The church of Saint Martin in the

Fields,' Simon supplied. His arms tightened about her limbs. 'I asked the wife of the innkeeper for a trysting place and she told me of these meadows.'

'You did not!' said Alice, torn between giggling and shock.

Simon lowered his head and waggled his black eyebrows at her. 'Hush, we do not want to disturb other lovers bedded here in these grasses.' Suddenly he looked younger, uncertain. 'We can return to the inn, if you wish.'

In answer, she took his head between her hands and kissed him.

This time she led and he followed. She lay on top of him, kissing him, smoothing her hands through his black curls and over his muscled arms and torso. 'You are so beautiful,' she told him, untying his tunic laces and kissing his cool, now warming skin. 'No, let me.'

She pressed him to the grass, plucked a flower and teased him with it, loving the way his eyes followed the nodding corn cockle, loving the way he snared her once, kissed her and lay back, trusting her.

'You are very bold, my lady,' he said to her, as she slowly peeled off his braies, unveiling his sinewy, long body. 'Was it wise for you to indulge in three cups of sweet wine this evening?'

Three cups give me a courage I might otherwise find too tricky to maintain. She licked and nipped his stomach, too shy even now to meet his eyes. 'If I cannot be bold with my husband, then who may I seduce?'

He chuckled, a dark, lovely sound. 'Seduce away, sweeting.' He clasped his hands behind his head, stretching out flat for her to do with him as she wished. Exposed and fully naked as he was, she could see every battle scar and wound that marred his lean, agile shape, but when she finally plucked up sufficient confidence to look him in the face, his blue eyes held only love and peace.

This is also our wedding night, she thought, a different wedding time from our last union, a secret, private night, just for us. Realizing the possibilities, she smiled back at him. *This is our time*. She nuzzled his throat, tonguing his big life vein, and sensed him swallowing. Raising her head again she stared into his craggy, smiling face, alive with emotion and all for her.

'My champion,' she murmured, patting his stubble with a finger.

'My bride,' he answered, clearly catching and appreciating the moment and mood as she did. He soared up afresh to offer and to take a kiss, lingering so lusciously that Alice felt her head would spin. 'Sweeter than strawberries,' he whispered, when they finally broke a little apart. His black brows furrowed, but not in complaint. 'Is that a new way with your hair, little wife, more up and back? It looks good, most queenly.'

Delighted, Alice tilted her nose in the air to be admired anew. As she lifted herself to preen, she accidentally jabbed her elbow into his stomach.

'Oof! Heed where you put yourself, Alice!' But he was grinning as he spoke and he tickled her beneath her breasts and under her arms until she collapsed, giggling against him. 'Now let me see more of this hair.'

He dragged off her head-rail, scattering the pins. 'Lovely,' he said. He stroked her shining, moon-lit locks, sweeping his hand from the crown of her head to her back and lower, deftly untying her simple gown. His warm hands coaxed and cupped her, gliding her clothes away as if each tie, ribbon, wool and linen was no more than a mist. 'You are so lovely, Alice, so lovely altogether, my English rose, rose and tawny and glowing.'

His loving earnestness transformed him, made him whole and unshadowed by his past. His words and his touch healed her, also, so Alice felt complete and accepted in a way she had never known before, except when she and Simon had been in bed together. *This is what love is. And Simon feels it, too, I know.*

'*Kyria*,' he growled softly against her ear.

He had said that before, on their first wedding night. 'What?' she whispered.

'It means 'Lady' in Greek.'

Her toes curled at the endearment. 'Am I your lady?' she teased, wanting him to say it.

The gleam in his eyes deepened. 'You are, little nag, and more. You are all.'

He kissed her fiercely, but she was not done yet. 'Tell me,' she prompted. 'Teach me to say, 'I love you,' in Greek.'

Simon tugged her lightly on top of him and said a few words, exotic and strange. She listened to his heart and felt the rumbling phrases die away, felt him breathe with her. Slowly, stumbling slightly over the words, she said the phrase back to him.

'Ah, Alice!' He hugged her, almost crushing her with his arms, but she did not care. She reveled in his embrace and, greatly daring, repeated the phrase.

He nipped her earlobe. 'Are you trying to tempt me, wench?'

'Yes, and I am succeeding,' she answered pertly, wriggling her hips against his big hands as he fondled her rump. His lingering caress against her naked skin woke the new, urgent hunger in her loins, that sweet burning. 'More,' she hissed, raising herself upward, to him.

This time she would be satisfied and well-pleasured, Simon swore to himself, skimming and stroking his fingers over her bottom, between her thighs. Pale and flawless as the finest glass, ghosted silver by the moon, she remained an endless miracle to him, an English miracle, his Alice. Nubile and slim, with flesh as white and pink as English apple blossom; delicate and strong. She shifted over and under his hands, receiving his caresses with unbridled delight, with a lusty passion that blasted away his previous doubts. *She wants me. She wants this, with me.* Better yet, her narrow fingers explored and gave delight in turn.

There was no fear here, no grim trouble, no memory or smell of burning or ruin, only his wife's sweet scent and her sweeter cries. Abruptly her pretty face colored to a deep rose and she flung her arms around his neck, clinging to him. He stroked the soft, plump folds between her thighs with faster, longer passes. She shuddered and her body bowed upwards, a breathy, drawn-out sob, half-triumph, half-yielding, calling to him, an invitation and challenge older than language.

'Me,' she said, when she could speak. 'Let me.'

Such joy, such sweet, wild joy. She could bask and bake in it all night, taking from Simon but bestowing, too. Alice saw the gladness in his face at her unabashed responses, knew the loving warrior in him had risen up to charge in turn, convinced now that the loving warrior in her was ready to dance. *We have healed each other*. Beautiful, jubilant, she knew nothing was impossible.

He gasped then as she kissed him intimately, on his full, thick manhood, stiffening half in clear rapture, half in shock. 'Alice, please . . . ' He bunched his hands into his scattered clothes. 'Please.'

Still in this heady moment he gave her control, waited for her to do what she wanted. He made her feel beautiful and powerful and loving. Slowly, she straddled him, glancing at his face. He was taut, every sinew ready and waiting. Savoring him, his long, muscled hardness, she sank onto him, feeling him full and snug within her. Deeper she eased and guided him, until they were joined hipbone to hipbone, and she watched him through every inch of pleasure. The hard, lean planes of his handsome face seem to ripple and melt, shimmering with tension, desire and need.

'Alice,' he begged, his mouth slack as if he could scarcely control himself, 'Alice — '

She was too generous a lady to deny him, her champion. 'Hold on,' she murmured, her teeth clenched as she remained determined not to rush, though her heart was hammering and the itch in her loins was both unbearable and delicious. Moving carefully at first and then more surely, she rocked them both. Dimly, through her own silvered joy, she heard Simon cry out her name, felt him quicken and pound faster within her, wonderfully hard and fast, flinging them into a panting, dazzling release.

Sated, overwhelmed, content, she dived into a foggy, gentle sleep like a swimmer into a warm pool, feeling Simon's arms cradling her, hearing his deep whisper, 'I love you so much, my Alice, my wife.'

And I you, my husband, she thought, and slept.

12

Simon woke long before dawn, savoring the feel of the supple, dainty body curled against his beneath his cloak. Again he had slept without nightmares. He knew he might have bad dreams in the future but with Alice in his bed he had a comfort and a confidant.

'She loves me, too.' He spoke the words aloud, for the wonder of it. He felt it in how she touched him, saw it in how she looked at him, heard it in how she spoke with him. *Even in our quarrels we reach for each other with our minds, trying to find common ground.* 'I am a lucky man.'

'Of course you are.' Stirring, Alice reached groggily for his water flask and jabbed him accidentally in the ribs, a sweetly clumsy touch about which he said nothing. She took a sip and offered him the flask. 'What is that smell? Like wet salt.'

'The sea. The Thames is close to the sea here.'

'What is it like, the sea? When you sailed, were you seasick?'

Interested, she sat up and he found himself too distracted by her pert breasts to make a sensible reply. 'I forget,' he mumbled.

She rubbed her eyes, still too endearingly sleepy to pick him up on his answer. 'Do you think we should go back?' Unaware of his delighted confusion, Alice stretched her arms above her head and he admired his nubile wife afresh, not caring even when she flicked his nose with a finger, saying, 'Listen, sleepy — '

He touched her mouth with his thumb and instantly she was silent. She too must have heard the jingle of a harness, the snorting breath of a horse ridden hard.

'Stay hidden.' Wide awake now and without troubling with his clothes, Simon reached for his sword. Crouching low, he pushed through the tall grasses and rose to his feet again beside the track that people used to walk to the church of Saint Martin. Lit by the rising sun, he stared along the green road.

Quietly, disobeying him, Alice dressed, gathered his clothes and moved toward the road herself.

'Simon Paton the mercenary. I should have guessed.' Speaking, the rider came into view and Alice smothered a gasp of recognition. He was low in the saddle and wide, a half-smile playing across his loose-lipped mouth. His eyes were as cold as a spring frost.

Simon held up his sword, its lethal tip pointing directly at the horse's heart. 'How did you find us, Bohemond?'

'Sir Bohemond, if you please, and I did not know you were involved. I thought I was seeking two silly girls. I've just ridden to the Bell Inn because Edward brought one of them to the inn last month and maidens do like to revisit trysting places. I hoped to recover her there and scoop up her sister as well.'

Bohemond paused, his small, greedy eyes darting here and there, looking beyond Simon. 'The sister has come to London, has she not?' he asked, and Alice prayed that the tall grasses hid her.

'You are a liar,' answered Simon, with seeming cheerfulness. 'You have just come from the Bell Inn because that is where you are staying and now you and your men are on the search again.'

The Bell. Staying at the Bell. They were so close to us at the Rose Inn and now they seek me and Henrietta. Alice shuddered at the thought, but Simon merely flicked his sword, making the blade shimmer and sparkle with deadly intent.

'Where is Edward?' he demanded.

'Still kicking his heels in the palace of Westminster, for all I know.' Bohemond reined in. 'Where are they, the women? My men are close. If you tell me I will let you live.'

Tell him! Alice's heart clamored within her. She almost flung herself out of the cover of the wild barley and field

144

flowers, revealing herself to save Simon, but her husband, naked as a champion of ancient Greece, was still as cool as glass.

'Lies again, man,' he answered scornfully. 'Your rabble would have attacked already. Get off your horse and come at me. We should settle this.'

'Ha!' Keeping low in the saddle, Bohemond dug his spurs into his horse and charged, straight at Simon. There was a crash of bright metal, a whirl of arms, the scream of the horse. Simon dropped his sword, seized the smaller, writhing man by the throat, and dragged him out of his stirrups.

'Mercy!' yelled Bohemond, as Alice, still gripping Simon's clothes, ran onto the track in time to see her husband hurl his adversary to the ground and kick Bohemond brutally in the balls. With a whimper, clawing desperately at his privates, the stocky Norman dropped into the dust.

'Bastard!' he moaned, coughing now on hands and knees. 'No honor.'

'I fight as a mercenary,' replied Simon calmly.

'And as my husband.' Alice stepped forward and swept his cloak over him. 'Will you spare him, my lord, as a favor to me?'

Simon retrieved his sword and only then turned his glittering blue eyes toward her, his harsh face seemingly cast in steel, but now his free hand clasped hers, gave her fingers a gentle squeeze.

He glanced at the still-choking Bohemond. ''tis a small favor, my Alice.'

'My Alice?' wheezed Bohemond. 'That sparrow-drab — ?'

He got no further in the insult. Simon smashed his fist into the man's face and Bohemond dropped a second time, unconscious, into the dust.

'Now do we take his horse and go home?' Alice asked. 'After you have dressed, that is.'

'Little nag!' Simon opened his cloak and she entered gladly into his arms.

'It is over, is it not?' she murmured. 'We can leave?'

'We can go,' he agreed. 'And right gladly, for me.'

They embraced for a long time, with the early sounds of a stirring London floating over the fields and the sweet promise of their homecoming to follow.

THE END

We do hope that you have enjoyed reading this large print book.

Did you know that all of our titles are available for purchase?

We publish a wide range of high quality large print books including:
Romances, Mysteries, Classics
General Fiction
Non Fiction and Westerns

Special interest titles available in large print are:
The Little Oxford Dictionary
Music Book, Song Book
Hymn Book, Service Book

Also available from us courtesy of Oxford University Press:
Young Readers' Dictionary
(large print edition)
Young Readers' Thesaurus
(large print edition)

For further information or a free brochure, please contact us at:
Ulverscroft Large Print Books Ltd.,
The Green, Bradgate Road, Anstey,
Leicester, LE7 7FU, England.
Tel: (00 44) **0116 236 4325**
Fax: (00 44) **0116 234 0205**

GIRL WITH A GOLD WING

Jill Barry

It's the 1960s, and Cora Murray dreams of taking to the skies — so when her father shows her a recruitment advertisement for air hostesses, she jumps at the chance to apply. Passing the interview with flying colours, she throws herself into her training, where she is quite literally swept off her feet by First Officer Ross Anderson. But whilst Ross is charming and flirtatious, he's also engaged — and Cora's former boyfriend Dave is intent on regaining her affections . . .

THE SURGEON'S MISTAKE

Chrissie Loveday

Matti Harper has been in love with Ian Faulkner since their school days. He is now an eminent cardiac surgeon, she his theatre nurse. Ian has finally fallen in love — the trouble is, it's with Matti's flatmate Lori! But whilst a heartbroken Matti prepares to be their bridesmaid, Lori is being suspiciously flirtatious with another man. How can Matti tell Ian without appearing to be jealous? Best man Sam Grayling tries to help, but only succeeds in sending things from bad to worse . . .

DANCE OF DANGER

Evelyn Orange

Injured ballet dancer Sonia returns to her family home, Alderburn Hall, to discover that her cousin Juliette is dead. Clues point to Lewis, Juliette's widower, being responsible — yet Sonia still finds herself falling in love with him . . . Several mysterious 'accidents' threaten not only her, but also Lewis's small daughter. Is Sonia in true danger? Can she discover the culprit? And can she and Lewis ever count on a future together?

THE UNFORGIVING HEART

Susan Udy

When wealthy businessman Luke Rivers asks Alex Harvey to utilise her specialist skills and decorate parts of his newly purchased home, she is determined to refuse. For this is the man who was responsible for practically destroying her family, something she can never forgive — or forget. Events, however, conspire against her in the shape of her demanding and increasingly rebellious younger brother Ricky and, despite her every instinct warning against it, she finds herself doing exactly what Luke Rivers wants . . .

AUGUSTA'S CHARM

Valerie Holmes

Attending her stepfather's dinner, Augusta is surprised to find that all the guests are single men. She quickly realises that she is being offered to the highest bidder. Faced with few options, Augusta finds herself leaving her home with Mr Benjamin Rufus Blood, destined for a life in Australia. However, there is far more adventure to be encountered en route. With her maid by her side, Augusta has to rely on more than just her charm to face the unknown future.

A FEAST OF SONGS

Patricia Keyson

In an act of kindness, Ellie offers to look after her friend's great aunt Phyllis after she suffers a fall. She travels to East Anglia and is entranced by the seaside town of Fairsands as well as the handsome and charming shopkeeper and restaurateur, Joe. Instead of the relaxing time she was hoping for, though, Ellie finds herself the target of acts of sabotage. Thinking revenge is the motive, she suspects Joe's former girlfriend Amber. But is she really a *former* girlfriend . . . ?